THE ROCK BOYZ 3

Money, Power, & Respect

TWYLA T.   PATRICE BALARK
DANI LITTLEPAGE   J. DOMINIQUE

The Roc Boyz 2: Money. Power. Resepct.

❀ Created with Vellum

This series is dedicated to our wonderful supporters! If it wasn't for you all, we would be reading our own work. Thanks for supporting us!!

"Ya---Yas--Yasmine." J.R. stuttered, staring into the eyes of his *dead* sister.

HE STOOD THERE FROZEN, FEET GLUED TO THE GROUND AS he tried to wrap his mind around her presence.

"CAN I COME IN BEFORE HE COMES BACK?" SHE LOOKED back nervously and asked.

"WHO? BEFORE *WHO* COMES BACK?" J.R. QUIZZED, PULLING his little sister inside and locking the door behind her.

"JU---JUSTIN." SHE WHISPERED, LOOKING DOWN AT THE ground.

J.R. TOOK A FEW STEPS BACK AND EXAMINED HIS SISTER. Growing up, Yasmine was always the pretty chubby girl with the round fat face, but the woman standing in front of him was unrecognizable.

"YOU GOOD? THEY HURT YOU?" HE ASKED, GRABBING HER by the hand and taking a look at her finger.

"OH, MY RING.... JUSTIN TOOK THAT FROM ME, AND I STILL have no clue as to why." She explained, looking down at her naked finger.

J.R.'S HEAD BEGAN SPINNING; HE HAD NEVER BEEN *SO confused* in his life. The entire time, he thought Yasmine was *dead* or somewhere with a *missing* ring finger, yet here she was, alive, well, and with all her limbs.

"WAIT. WAIT. WAIT... THIS SHIT TOO MUCH. YASMINE tell me what happened, from the beginning." He requested.

YASMINE LOOKED AROUND FIRST BEFORE LETTING OUT A long sigh. It was clear that she was puzzled and shaken up as well but J.R. needed answers.

"YOU GOOD. YOU SAFE NOW. TELL ME WHAT HAPPENED?" he asked again.

"I WAS KICKING IT WITH THIS GUY I MET ON FACEBOOK. He asked me if I wanted to go shopping so I said cool. After the mall, he took me back to this big ass house, which he said belonged to his cousin. Once there, they started smoking, popping pills, and drinking. They offered it all to me, but I declined.... Fast forward, I woke up in a basement and been there ever since." She explained.

J.R. REMAINED QUIET FOR A WHILE, PIECING THE PUZZLE together in his head and even after hearing Yasmine's story, he was still lost.

"OK, WHO IS JUSTIN?" HE QUIZZED.

"*YOUR* FATHER." SHE LOOKED HIM IN THE EYES AND replied.

J.R. WANTED TO SEE HOW MUCH YASMINE KNEW BUT EVEN after his discovery, he had no idea how she was standing in front of him.

"OK LOOK BABY GIRL, START FROM THE TOP." HE STATED, running his hands over his beard, getting a bit frustrated.

"I TOLD YOU..... WHEN I HAD COMPANY WITHOUT YOUR permission, one of the dudes here must have known who you were. Word got back to Tessa's cartel that I was your sister, so they snatched me up but then shit went left. I was kept in this basement for about a day before anyone even acknowledged that I was there. One day out the blue, two men dressed in suits came down to talk to me. One of the dudes was heavy set with a mole on his face..."

As J.R. LISTENED, HE QUICKLY KNEW THAT THE MAN Yasmine was describing was Elliot, the brother who they killed at the motel.

"I REMEMBER HE HAD THIS *SICK* LOOK IN HIS EYES. THE WAY he looked at me made chill bumps form on my body. Anyway, the next dude was the complete opposite. He was calm, well-spoken, and he looked *exactly* like you." She paused and locked eyes with J.R.

NODDING HIS HEAD IN AGREEMENT, HE MOTIONED FOR HER to continue, so she did.

"THE FAT NIGGA WANTED TO JUST KILL ME RIGHT AWAY, BUT Justin, wanted answers. At that time, they only knew you as one of the niggas from the Rock Boyz but once they started talking, shit began to unfold...... Ok, so they got me in this basement and Justin came straight out and asked who my brother was. At first, I wouldn't tell them but then the fat one started punching me and......"

YASMINE BROKE DOWN AND CRIED AS SHE REMINISCED ON the time she spent away. J.R. pulled his sister closer to him and hugged her tight.

"IT'S ALL OVER, THAT NIGGA GONE NOW," HE SAID, RUBBING her back as she wept in his arms.

AFTER A FEW MORE MINUTES OF REASSURING, YASMINE wiped her face and continued the story.

"I TOLD THEM YOUR NAME, BUT I TOLD THEM *J.R.* AND OF course, it didn't ring a bell, so they thought I was lying to them. The fat one get to talking about..... *"Tessa this and the Tessa Cartel that"* and it rung a bell. I remembered *Tessa* was the last name on your birth certificate, so I put two and two together and asked how they knew your last name. When I said that, the both of them froze and stared at me. Of course, the fat one spazzed even more while Justin began to ask questions. He asked more in-depth questions like your real name, birthday and shit like that..... I'm so sorry J.R., I started telling him everything because I was scared," she cried.

J.R. PULLED YASMINE IN CLOSER AND CONSOLED HER AGAIN.

"LOOK, IT'S COOL. FINISH TALKING," HE URGED HER.

"JUSTIN MADE THE OTHER DUDE LEAVE. HE THEN GRABBED a chair and sat in front of me. He was so intrigued with everything I had to say about you. It wasn't until he asked about mom that changed the mood for me. I told him she passed away and J.R. I swear to God, he had the same look in his eyes that you had at her funeral. It was *so scary*. He even knew about when I was born and that's when he confirmed that he was your dad. After that, he made me give him my ring but promised I would get it back. He then snuck me out that basement and took me to this other house where he kept me. Justin made sure I ate, he even made sure I had a TV to watch, but he always kept someone around the clock watching me."

"LIKE FATHER LIKE SON." J.R. MUMBLED TO HIMSELF AS HE thought about how he did the same thing with Jessica.

"OK, SO HOW YOU END UP HERE?" J.R. QUESTIONED.

"HE DROPPED ME OFF. I HEARD SOME OF HIS GUYS TALKING and apparently one of his brothers was shot and killed today, and he thinks *you* had something to do with it." She replied.

DURING THE SHOOTOUT AT THE CEMETERY, J.R. WASN'T sure whether or not Grant actually took a hit because bodies and bullets were flying everywhere, but Yasmine had just confirmed it. J.R. was happy to hear that but couldn't celebrate because now D'Mari was fighting for his life.

"I'M SO SORRY YOU HAD TO GO THROUGH THIS BULLSHIT AT the hands of me, but I swear to God on mommy's grave that no one will *ever* touch you again." J.R. assured his little sister.

YASMINE NODDED HER HEAD UP AND DOWN AS TEARS slowly streamed down her face. J.R. needed Yasmine to understand that his word was bond and that no one else he loved would ever be harmed again. The Rock Boyz took a few losses but now it was over. J.R. had all he needed now to end this shit, *for good.*

"LET'S GET YOU HOME. COME ON," HE SAID, USHERING HER off towards the door but Yasmine wouldn't move her feet.

"WHAT'S WRONG? LET'S GO!" HE SAID AGAIN, THIS TIME NO longer pushing her.

"BEFORE WE GO, JUSTIN HAD A MESSAGE FOR YOU AND I need to tell you," she said softly, her voice trembling.

J.R. STOOD THERE SILENTLY, WAITING FOR HER TO SPEAK but instead, she just stared at him, scared.

"OK LOOK, YOU CAN TELL ME IN THE CAR, LET'S GO!" HE urged, this time showing his frustration.

J.R. MOVED AROUND YASMINE AND TOWARDS THE DOOR first. He held it open for her as she slowly stepped onto the front porch. Just as J.R. was about to close and lock the door, shots rang out as a car flew down the street, sending bullets their way. J.R. swiftly jumped on top of Yasmine, knocking her into the ground, shielding her until the shots stopped.

"YOU GOOD? YOU GOOD?" HE ASKED FRANTICALLY.

"YES," SHE REPLIED, CLEARLY SHAKEN UP.

"LET'S GO!"

J.R. GRABBED YASMINE'S HAND AND PULLED HER TO THE car. Once inside, he wasted no time cranking it up and peeling off. Once he was a few miles away, he looked over to check on Yasmine who just stared ahead out the front window.

"YOU THINK THAT WAS HIM?" J.R. ASKED, REFERRING TO Justin.

"NO. I KNOW FOR A FACT IT *WASN'T* HIM," SHE REPLIED, turning her head in his direction.

"AND HOW YOU KNOW?" J.R. QUIZZED WITH A LIFTED eyebrow.

"I KNOW BECAUSE JUSTIN SAID HE WOULD NEVER HURT YOU and he's a man of his word... and when the window rolled down, *that* shooter looked a lot like *our* cousin Julian."

"Don't you die on me man... I got you! Ima get you to the hospital!" Mari heard J.R. saying. He wished that he could open his eyes up and talk back, but he couldn't do it for shit. Mari dozed in and out of consciousness as J.R. drove to the hospital. The dream that he had when Drea got shot eased into his mind and sent him into a panic. Instead of waking up like he so desperately tried to do, he found himself walking towards a white light.

"African American male... late twenties to early thirties... multiple gunshot wounds... we have to remove the one that's located near his aorta ASAP... his BP is dropping and we have to do surgery right away!"

"Is the next of kin present? We need permission to proceed."

"We really don't have any time to waste. This is one of those situations where we have to make a judgment call because we're going to lose him if we don't start right now!"

"Got it doc... we're ready. I'll get him sedated now."

Those were the last words D'Mari heard before the doctors and nurses started talking in medical terms and injected something in him before he drifted off.

❀

No matter how hard Mari tried to wake up, he just couldn't. He didn't know how long he had been out. All Mari knew was that people had been in and out checking on him and he had even heard Drea crying and rubbing his hands. D'Mari couldn't help but to think about their arguments and the thought of not making up with her made him fight harder to try to wake up.

"Baby please wake up. I'm so sorry. I swear I never cheated on you. I've been working on a case and it's confidential. Eventually, I was gonna tell you, but I thought that I could handle everything on my own. *That* Janice bitch is *crazy*. She tried to kill her husband and he..."

Mari listened to his wife tell him about why she had been acting so suspicious. He wanted to wake up and tell her that he understood and everything was going to be alright, but he couldn't. A nurse walked in and she started talking to Drea; however, she spoke barely above a whisper so he couldn't hear what she was saying. A few seconds later, they walked out and he heard his brothers' voices next. Corey and Mani told him to get his ass up. They were joking, but he could hear the seriousness and concern in their voices. Their voices eventually wore off and Mari drifted off to sleep.

❀

D'Mari woke up in a coughing fit the next day and Drea jumped up from beside him and yelled for the nurse.

"He's awake... nurse he's awake!" she screamed as she squeezed his hand.

"Baby... I'm so glad you're awake. Hold on, they're coming," Drea cried and hugged Mari.

He felt her tears when they hit his face and chest. Even

though he was in pain, he was glad to have her by his side. The doctor and nurse rushed into the room and then started checking Mari's vitals. It wasn't until he tried to talk that he realized a tube was down his throat. The nurse must have noticed his panic because she spoke to him in an attempt to calm him down.

"It's okay. We'll remove that shortly. That's why you had a coughing fit when you came back around," she explained.

The nurse asked Drea to step out of the room and she tried to put up a fuss, but she obliged once the nurse told her that they were trying to save her husband's life.

"You're going to feel a little pain as we remove this tube, but it will only last a few seconds," the doctor explained.

A few minutes and a hundred questions later, Drea was finally allowed back in the room. Mari was told that patients like him who had suffered the exact same injuries were either paralyzed or dead. He was very grateful that he was still alive, but he knew what he needed to tell Drea wasn't going to go over to well, so he said a silent prayer that she didn't kill him right then and there. After taking another sip of water, he looked into his wife's eyes and gave her hand a tight squeeze.

"I need to tell you something," she broke the silence.

"No... don't worry bout it. I just wanna apologize for everything. I know this shit ain't easy to deal wit, plus you got a life and a career too. You handling all that shit like *the boss* you are and I appreciate you. I need you to do something... I know you not gonna agree, but it's not really up for debate. You, your sisters, and all the kids gon' have to go to Mississippi while we handle this sh..."

"I'm not leaving you D'Mari... I'm not gon' be five hours away worried sick and waiting on a phone call abo..."

"Drea, this ain't really up for debate. Think about the kids," Mari cut her off.

"Well... our moms and the kids can go, but me and my

sisters are staying here," Drea folded her arms across her chest.

Mari laid there in thought as he stared at his wife. He never expected her to even agree to the kids leaving; so since she did, he told himself that he had to at least compromise. He didn't want any of them there because the Rock Boyz were about to paint the whole state *red*, not just the fuckin' city, but maybe the women could indirectly help them out.

"We'll talk about it... I gotta get outta here," Mari said and sat up.

"D'Mari you're not leaving here until they discharge you," Drea fussed.

Before he could reply, the door flew open and some of the family piled in.

"Boy you wanna be the third Tupac so bad!" Aunt Shirley was the first one to talk, making everyone laugh.

All of the women told Mari how glad they were that he was okay. His mom cried and then cussed him out for scaring her. That was the main reason they needed the women and children gone; they were too emotional. Just when Mari was about to ask where the guys were, in walked J.R. and Mani and he could tell by the looks on their faces that something else was terribly wrong. Mani walked over and showed him a text message on his phone and Mari's heart dropped.

3

S hit just keep going from bad to worse. D'Mani thought sullenly. Not only had Cheyanne died, but she died the *exact* same night his brother had been fighting for his life. Although D'Mari managed to pull through, they weren't out of the clear though, just yet. He was in the middle of explaining to Imani that her mother had died the previous night when he'd gotten the picture text of Corey beaten the fuck up and with his hands and feet tied.

Him and JR had shown D'Mari the text, but they weren't able to go into too much detail since the women were all in the room, and they knew Drea had no intentions on leaving his side anytime soon. To avoid drawing the sisters' suspicions, they figured the best course of action would be to just text each other, but that was easier said than done with everyone in the same room. They were all pretty preoccupied with other shit, but if the sisters noticed them all into their phones typing away that would definitely draw their attention.

D'Mani sat in the corner with Imani in his lap and Stasia at his side running her hand over his waves. She was being extra touchy at the moment and he knew it was mostly because of everything that was going on. He usually wouldn't have minded, but under the circumstances, he felt like he couldn't open his phone up with her over his shoulder since there was no telling what might pop up.

"Hey, umm... where's Corey?" that was Alyssa, and at the mention of his name, all of the men looked at each other. They hadn't had a chance to talk about shit, so they didn't know what they would tell her about her husband's where-abouts when she asked. She eyed them all suspiciously when they didn't answer right away. "I've been texting and calling him, but it's going straight to voicemail. I thought he was with y'all since he never brought my stuff back from the store."

Since D'Mari had been up in the hospital since the night before, her question was more so directed towards JR and D'Mani. Their silence had everyone's eyes landing on either him or JR and D'Mani hurried to think of a quick lie that would suffice.

"Uh, we had to send him on a last minute run to Mexico to meet with the connect," he told her quickly and from the frown that covered her face, he knew more questions were coming.

"Y'all sent him alone?"

"Shiiit... he safer where he at than being back here with us," JR answered from his spot next to Lexi. "He probably still at dude's house and we can't take phones in there."

"Yeah I'm sure he'll call you later," D'Mani added before she could say anything else.

"Oooookaaaay," she dragged out with narrowed eyes. "I'm gonna go try him again and see if he answers this time."

As soon as she left out, an uncomfortable silence fell over the room until D'Mari sparked up a conversation with Drea about the twins. Although the mood lightened a little bit,

14

D'Mani was sure that they would eventually have questions, especially if Corey didn't pop up in the next few days. That suspicion was confirmed when Alyssa came back into the room with a disappointed look on her face.

"Damn, you still ain't talk to him?" Lexi asked when she saw her sister's demeanor.

"Naw, not yet, but maybe he's still busy. I'll just try again later." D'Mani instantly felt bad about what was going on, but it was in their best interests to not know right away. They had already been through so much and telling them about Corey would only add to their stress. Plus, they didn't have anything to tell them yet anyway, all he had was a damn picture text from some random number. "I'm about to take the baby home y'all, it's getting pretty late."

"Yeah, I think we should be heading out too, this baby bouta make my arm fall asleep," Lexi complained jokingly, causing JR to look at her sideways.

"Quit playin' with my lil dude, yo ass the one that insist on holdin' him when his car seat right there," he pointed out.

"You really gone try and bust me out though?" she pretended to be offended because they all knew that she loved holding him. "You want me to take the twins?"

"Yeah, I'll stay up here again tonight, hopefully they'll be letting him go home tomorrow." Drea told her grabbing up the babies bag so she could get them ready to go.

"I'ma head out too bro." D'Mani stood to give his brother a pound with Imani still clinging to him. "We gone holla at you later about that other shit." D'Mari nodded his understanding, knowing that they needed to talk about the next course of action as far as finding Corey.

After saying their goodbyes, him and Anastasia left the hospital right after Lexi with Aunt Shirley and Alyssa in tow. His mind ran a mile a minute on the drive back to the house as he tried to figure out who could've taken Corey and how they would go about getting him back. Whoever it was had yet to send him another text despite the two that he had sent asking what they wanted. D'Mani wasn't used to kidnapping situations, but he was sure that they wanted something and that usually they would have already called with their demands. Not knowing and having to walk a fine line was putting him more on edge than he already was.

"Baby you okay?" Anastasia asked, placing her hand in his on the console. D'Mani nodded silently.

"Hell naw he ain't okay!" Shirley shouted from the back. "He one down, shit! If I don't get the chance to tell you, I'm sorry for your loss pimpin'!"

"Aunty Shirley, now is not the time," Anastasia said and put her face in her hands while Alyssa gasped from the back-seat. At that point, D'Mani wasn't even surprised by some of the shit that came out of their Aunt's mouth. He really ain't know how they were always so shocked when she said something crazy. Knowing that it was just the liquor talking as usual, he just shook his head as they pulled into the driveway beside JR's car. He could hear Anastasia fussing at her as he walked around so that he could grab a sleeping Imani out of Alyssa's lap and gently wake up Kyler.

"Y'all heffas always tryna check me! I'm grown... I can say what I want out my mouth! I swear y'all startin' to act more and more like y'all judgmental ass daddy!" Shirley waved them off and headed inside with everyone behind her.

"I'm so sorry about that... I-."

"It's cool Stasia... I ain't trippin' off yo Aunty," D'Mani cut her off and went in the house to lay Imani down.

After putting baby girl to bed and showering, he sent a quick message to JR to meet in the basement since he wasn't sure of where he was in the house. As soon as he got into their "man cave," he poured him a shot and downed it quickly before pouring another. By the time JR entered the room, the drinks had done their job and knocked the edge off for the time being. Of course, with the conversation that loomed, he was sure it wouldn't be for long though.

"Nigga don't be textin' me no shit like meet you in the basement at eleven at night. That shit sounded gay as hell! I started not to even come down here!" J.R. snapped, checking to make sure the door was locked behind him.

"Shit, what did you want me to do? Slip a note under your door? I called myself tryna be discrete!"

"I don't give a fuck if you gotta send me a smoke signal nigga... that shit suspect as hell! Now I gotta keep my fuckin' eye on you."

D'Mani waved him off and then filled another shot glass before taking a seat in the recliner.

"Man fuck you!" he grumbled, putting D'Mari's number into his phone. Once it started ringing, he put it on speaker and then placed it on the coffee table.

"Aye we gone have to make this quick. I sent Drea to go get some ice cream from one of these nurses," D'Mari came on the line talking fast.

"Ayite, well you seen the text. You think it's bullshit?" D'Mani questioned unsure about how far whoever it was, was willing to take it.

"Even if it is bullshit, can we really afford to play games, shit? They already fucked him up, ain't no tellin what else they might do. Did they send anything else?"

"Hell nah but that's what's makin' me not really wanna believe this shit. How come them niggas ain't asked for shit yet, like what the fuck they tryna get for him?"

"Listen, I'm takin' *every* threat to heart no matter the circumstances... so if niggas out here snatchin' muthafuckas up then we need to send the girls and kids away until we can figure this shit out," JR finally said.

"I agree."D'Mari voiced. "Shit been too crazy lately and I ain't tryna play around with my family's safety."

"Real shit." D'Mani nodded. They needed to keep the women out of harm's way and the best way to do that would be sending them all back to Mississippi and away from all the madness.

"Ayite so we gone let them know they leavin', and in the meantime, we need to be tryna follow any leads we can to Corey. Hopefully, them bitch ass niggas find the balls to ask us for what they want by tomorrow."

The men all agreed to talk again the next day so that they could further map out a course of action before saying their goodbyes and getting off the phone. JR went right upstairs after the call ended ready to get back to his family, but D'Mani remained, finding some solace in the dark and quiet basement. He had a lot of shit on his mind and had to keep up a brave front. Trying to juggle everything on his plate while simultaneously taking care of Cheyanne's remains were going to be a lot, but he had no doubt that he'd be able to pull it off.

4

The pain in Corey's body was excruciating as he sat tied up to a steel chair. The pounding in his head caused him to squeeze his eyes shut for long periods of time before opening them again. When the pain subsided a little, Corey opened his eyes and noticed that he was in a cold ass basement with a dim light and two chairs. He noticed the blood that stained his shirt and jeans and assumed that it had to come from his head. As he sat there, Corey tried to remember how the hell he got to where he was and when he thought about Alyssa, he cussed under his breath.

"I know Alyssa is probably tripping right now," he sighed.

Corey heard a door open and close from above and tried to sit up as straight as he could. Even though his body was in pain, he'd be damn if he gave the motherfuckers that snatched his ass up the satisfaction of knowing that he was. Corey refused to show any signs of weakness. The footsteps crossed the floor making their way to the basement door. Preparing himself to come face to face with a nigga, his jaws tightened at the sight of Deana's grinning face. Instead of showing his anger, Corey decided to not show any emotion.

"Well, look who's finally up?" She stood in front of him. "How are you feeling?"

Corey didn't speak.

"Being as though they fucked you up pretty bad, I know you must be in a lot of pain."

Again, he remained silent.

"I know you're probably wondering what I'm doing here and who I'm working with or why I would be a part of something like this after all we've been through," Deana took a seat in one of the chairs.

Corey let out a sigh of annoyance before she continued.

"I already know why. Ya ass is bitter because I dismissed ya ass. Even though I told ya ass what it was from the beginning, you made yaself believe that if you did everything I asked, I would allow you to be in my life in some form or fashion," he chuckled. "I thought ya ass was different but you're just like the rest of these ditzy bitches that can't stick to the script and not let their feelings get involved."

By the expression on Deana's face, he knew that he had struck a nerve. Her face was balled up and looked as if she was ready to fight. Getting up from the chair, she walked over to Corey, punching him in the face. That shit felt like a love tap.

"I'm not bitter. I'm just pissed because out of all the men that told me the same shit you did, you were the only one that stuck to that shit. Every time I set out to get a man, I *don't* fail. Regardless of what they say and even though you had a pregnant wife and all, I just knew I was going to get a chance to have you. Even if it was only a *one time* thing but I never got a chance. So yeah, I helped these niggas kidnap ya ass out of spite," she shrugged. "I hope you told ya wife and daughter that you loved them the last time you saw them because by the way these niggas talking, ya ass ain't making it out of here alive."

Sitting back down in the chair, Corey sat there in deep thought while Deana continued to annoy the fuck out of him by the conversation she was having on the phone. Besides thinking of the multiple ways he wanted to kill that bitch for playing a part in his kidnapping, he was thinking about his brothers and hoping that everyone was cool. He was supposed to ride out with them to handle one of the brothers but knowing how his brothers rolled, Corey was sure they were fine. He also thought about his daughter and how she was probably giving her mother hell because she hadn't seen him in God knows how long.

After her long ass conversation about nothing, Deana left him in the basement alone. Still in his thoughts, Corey assumed that the niggas that were holding him hostage had to be a part of the Tessa Cartel and they either wanted the location of his brothers, money, or both. If these niggas were expecting a positive outcome from this stunt, they were sadly mistaken. After staring at the same wall for hours, Corey drifted off to sleep. The slamming of the basement door caused him to jump awake. Two sets of heavy footsteps came down the basement stairs. When the two men stepped into the dim light, he couldn't believe who was standing in front of him.

"I see ya bitch ass finally woke up, huh?" Julian smirked, pulling one of the chairs closer to Corey before sitting down. "I can't believe this nigga was bold enough to kill some damn body. He don't even seem like he's built for this shit."

"None of us really know what we're capable of doing until we're force to do the unthinkable," Larry replied. "Besides, you should already know that you can't judge a book by the cover," he grabbed the other chair, sitting next to Julian.

Boiling over with anger, Corey couldn't believe that these

niggas were his kidnappers. The last time he saw Larry, their conversation ended on sour terms and when they discovered that Julian was dirty, his ass went into hiding. When Larry was signed out of rehab by his nephew, Corey figured that Julian had to be the one to do it since Julian called Larry his uncle. Since Julian setup J.R., he knew it was only a matter of time that he would try to strike again but not like this.

"It's a shame we have to meet under these circumstances Corey but after our last visit, I knew that any chance we had of becoming friends was nonexistent," Larry leaned forward. "I was hoping my generous approach would make things easier for me to ask a favor of you, but you saw through that shit and I have to admit that I was impressed. You didn't do a lot of talking and I had to do my research on you. When Julian here told me that you were a part of the Rock Boyz and that y'all were after the Tessa Cartel, I figure we could somehow work together to take them down since they're the ones responsible for my current status of life."

"What?"

"That's right. I used to be a part of the Tessa Cartel. Them niggas were like my family. We built that shit from the ground up and after dedicating my life to those ungrateful bastards for nearly thirty years, they give me the axe when shit starts going downhill and money starts missing. I even proved to them fuck niggas that I wasn't the one responsible for the mishaps that were taking place but they still cut me off," he yelled. "My life after the cartel caused me to slip into deep depression. I wanted to start an empire of my own but the Tessa brothers made sure nobody would work with or for my ass since I was labeled as a thief. The downward spiral of my life led me to the rehab," Larry spoke in low voice.

"And you thought just because you volunteered info that we were gonna join forces or some shit? You can't be the fuck serious?" Corey laughed.

"Everything comes with a price and since we couldn't handle this shit the easy way, if you don't choose to cooperate, this shit is gonna end deadly," Julian pulled the gun from his waist band.

"You motherfuckers don't scare me," Cory answered unfazed.

Julian stood to his feet, towering over Corey. The two men stared each other down before Julian knocked him unconscious with the butt of his gun.

5

J.R. took a hard pull from the blunt he was smoking before titling his head back, releasing the smoke in the air. It had been a few days since the shooting. With D'Mari being home, things were starting to calm down, minus the fact that Corey was still missing. Although it hadn't been confirmed yet, the guys were pretty sure that Julian and Larry were behind his disappearance; they just had yet to tie Julian and Larry's connection to each other. Thinking about the way his cousin betrayed him made J.R.'s blood boil. He introduced him to the guys, thinking he'll be an asset to the team, but he had done nothing but caused them more turmoil. A part of him wanted answers while the other part of him only wanted him dead.

"Aight y'all. I've reserved two Suburban trucks to drive the girls and kids to Mississippi in," Mani said, ending the call he was on with Enterprise.

"Aight bet. It's a five-hour drive. We make sure they are settled and then head back here, it shouldn't take too much time out of our day," Mari chimed in as he stood up slowly.

J.R. watched him limp over to the bar to pour himself a shot of *Patron*.

"If Drea see you drinking that with all the meds you already on, she'll have a fit," J.R. stated, shaking his head.

"Drea ain't gon' know shit, unless you snitching," D'Mari turned around and replied.

"Mannnn...... let dat nigga be great." D'Mani laughed as he too joined his twin at the bar.

"That's y'all motherfuck'n' problem, all y'all wanna do is drink," J.R. replied, taking another pull from the weed.

"And nigga, that's yo problem," the twins said in unison, causing J.R. to choke on the smoke.

J.R. wasn't much of a drinker but the weed calmed his nerves. It seemed like the only person who understood that was Aunt Shirley. Lexi smoked up until she found out she was pregnant and since she was breast feeding, she had yet to start back. J.R. lied to himself daily about how he was going to stop but he needed the reefa now more than ever. Just as J.R. was about to roll another blunt, he heard his name being called from upstairs. Letting out a long sigh, he stood to his feet and headed towards the stairs.

"Let me go see what this girl wants, I'll be back," he announced, dismissing himself.

J.R. headed up the stairs, only to find all four Holiday sisters sitting at the kitchen counter, eyeing him.

"Da fuck y'all looking at?" he quizzed, turning up his face.

"We need to talk to you," Lexi spoke up first, eyeing J.R. intensively.

"WE? About what?" he asked, walking over to the cabinet, grabbing a bag of chips, and opening them.

"Yeah... WE and because WE need answers." Andrea spoke up as the other three sisters chimed in with head nods.

J.R. stood there eating his chips as he waited to see what

was to come next. He tried his best to avoid eye contact, but they were staring holes through him.

"Aight. What y'all wanna know?" he asked, smacking on the last bit of crumbs.

"Ok, for starters. Where is my husband?" Alyssa asked.

"You know what? That's a good question, let me get that answer for you...... D'MARRIIIIII....... D'MANNNIIIII!" J.R walked to the basement door and called out.

There was no way in hell he was going to let them gang up on him, especially since he knew no more information than the other guys. As soon as the twins hit the top step, they both had the same look on their faces as J.R. had moments ago.

"Da fuck y'all looking at?" D'Mani asked, causing J.R. to burst out in laughter.

He abruptly stopped when he noticed the girls staring at him, their faces ridden with attitude.

"Aye, my bad," he quickly apologized, trying his best to regain his composure.

"Look. We all need answers, starting with where the fuck is Corey?" Anastasia finally spoke up, rolling her eyes at J.R. who still chuckled underneath his breath.

"We told y'all," D'Mari replied.

"Y'all told us some bullshit," Lexi snapped, she too rolled her eyes at J.R.

"Hold the fuck on. Y'all throwing all the heat my way like I'm responsible for every fucking thing," he barked.

"No, we not. We just want answers J.R., that's all." Alyssa assured him.

Lyssa was always the calm one when it came to the Holiday sisters, which was why the guilt of Corey's absence was weighing on him. The men knew they couldn't tell the women the truth, but they just had to prepare them for whatever was next.

"Listen, nothing has changed since we last told y'all about him handling business," D'Mari stepped in and spoke.

"What type of business that will keep him *away* from your wife and new child?" Lyssa asked softly.

Damn. Was J.R. thoughts as he watched Alyssa's eyes water. The fact of the matter was, they weren't sure themselves if they'll see Corey alive again. All of the guys hated lying to the women, but it was a choice they didn't have.

"Look y'all. We got shit under control. It's some shit going on in Mexico and we can't even get in touch with him, but we know for a fact that he's good," D'Mari lied.

J.R. scanned the faces of the girls to see if they were buying it but it was clear that they were not.

"Then like..... we really not gon' further discuss how the fuck Yasmine popped back up?" Drea chimed in.

"With her finger and all," Aunt Shirley walked in and added.

J.R. cut his eyes at their aunt before shaking his head.

"We told yawl all yawl needed to know. She was missing but she's good now," J.R. replied.

"You got me soooo fucked upppppp," Lexi grunted, scooting the chair back and standing to her feet.

"Y'all gotta think we stupid," Stasia chuckled.

"*Stupid* ain't the word, y'all niggas think y'all *dumb as fuck!*" Aunt Shirley laughed.

All three guys cut their eyes at her while the girls shook their head in agreement. Aunt Shirley talked too much but J.R. knew exactly how to shut her up; he knew how to silence them all.

"Look, we can continue this at a later date but right now, y'all need to pack," D'Mari stepped in and stated.

"Pack?"

"Pack for what?"

"Where the fuck we going?"

Lexi, Drea, and Stasia took their turns fussing but it fell on death ears. At this point, neither of them had a say-so, therefore, they were wasting their breath.

"Pack for what? I'm not going anywhere, especially while Corey is M.I.A," Lyssa chimed in.

"Lyssa, you ain't got no choice either. If they leaving, you leaving, ain't no way around it," J.R. told her.

"And exactly where y'all think we going?" Lexi folded her arms across her chest and asked.

"To Mississippi with the kids. Once everything on the up and up around here, we will send for y'all," D'Mari told the ladies.

The kitchen went into an uproar after those words were spoken. Each sister, including Shirley, fussed about leaving Atlanta but the plan was already in motion, and it wasn't shit neither of them could do about it.

❧ 6 ❧

"I'm not leaving D'Mari!!" Drea said as soon as she walked into the bedroom.

"Drea, it's not up for debate!" Mari boomed.

"But..."

"Ain't no buts babe... we got shit to handle and it's my job to protect my family and that's exactly what I'm gon' do."

Drea rolled her eyes, and Mari could tell by the look in her eyes that she had something else to say. It wouldn't be Drea if she didn't analyze a situation to death. Luckily for him, he had grown use to it.

"I understand you have to protect us babe... I really do, but I think y'all are lying about Corey. Why would y'all send him alone? Have you talked to him? Why didn't he at least tell Lyssa he had some business to handle instead of leaving to go to the store and never coming back? The shit just ain't adding up. I mean, I love Corey but the crackh... I mean he just got outta rehab and y'all trust him to go somewhere like that alone?" Drea spoke nonstop as she paced the floor.

"Drea baby... I need you to calm down and trust me," Mari got up and hugged her from behind.

"I'm just sayi..."

"Shhh... let me handle it. I just need you to take care of my babies and stay safe. Can you do that for me?" he kissed her neck.

"Yeah," she finally gave in.

Mari made a trail of kisses from the back of her neck to the front. Soft moans escaped her lips and Mari silenced those moans when his mouth met hers. He kissed her passionately. Tears began to run down Drea's cheeks and he kissed those away.

"I don't wanna leave you."

"I know baby. I don't you to leave, but it's for the best."

"We really could help y'all..."

"You can help me by giving me some of my pussy."

"Drea smirked at him and then pushed him down on the bed.

Mari had been out of the hospital for a couple of days, but the only thing she had did was gave him some fye head. Drea was afraid of hurting him. She had finally taken some personal time away from the office; in fact, she allowed an associate to handle everything for at least the next month. She eased down on his pole and they both moaned in pleasure.

"Shit baby... got damn! That's it... keep that shit up," Mari coaxed as Drea rode his dick like a stallion.

"Umm... You sure... I'm not...umm... hurting you? Drea moaned.

"Nah babe... don't stop."

Even though Mari was feeling a little bit of pain, there was no way he was about to tell her because he needed some pussy. That was his best stress reliever. Considering the status of their relationship before the shooting, Mari was just glad to have shit back on track. Drea had been catering to his every need ever since he woke up from surgery. She was being the *Andrea* that he had fallen in love with. It's crazy how shit went. They both had almost lost their lives in a matter of weeks, but it seemed like it had brought them closer together.

"Oh my gawwwdddd... I'm bout to cuummm bae!" Drea screamed.

"Let that shit go!"

As soon as the words left his mouth, he felt Drea's juices flow all over him. Mari made a quick move and flipped her off of him and dove headfirst into her pussy. He loved to taste her cum and wasn't about to let those juices go to waste.

"I can... can't take it baby! Shiiittt!"

"You want me to stop?" Mari quizzed, stopping momentarily.

"N...nooo!" Drea stuttered.

After she came again, Mari eased back inside of her, ignoring any pain he was feeling and hit her spot with every single stroke. A few minutes later, he filled her with his seeds and flopped down beside her.

Drea snuggled up close and Mari wrapped his arm around her. He was at total peace with his queen by his side and it was the perfect moment. They held each other until an unfamiliar voice fucked up their vibe.

"I bet y'all in their fuckin' too... come get these babies wit y'all crazy asses. Y'all believe anything these niggaz say... that's how I know y'all ain't my nieces," Aunt Shirley's voice trailed off down the hall as she talked.

"If she wasn't my auntie, I would really kick her ass," Drea said.

"That old lady will give you a run for ya money," Mari joked.

"Tuh... go get your kids since I gotta pack," Drea's attitude semi returned.

Mari kissed her on the forehead and dipped out to

prevent another argument. He went to the twin's room so that he could spend some time with them before shipping them out. Mari felt bad, but he knew that he was doing what was best and hoped that everything would go according to their plan.

7

D'Mani sat on the bed while Anastasia paced the floor in front of him mumbling under her breath. They had agreed that it would be best for the women to go back to Mississippi, but he knew they wouldn't be happy about it. Even as he watched her pacing and trying to figure out a way out of going back, he still was going to make her go. Right along with her sisters and all of the kids.

"Anastasia sit down. Runnin' a hole in the carpet ain't gone stop y'all from havin' to go," he told her, running a hand down his face.

"You really think us leavin' is gone do somethin'! What if the niggas y'all tryna keep us "safe" from bring their asses there and we're alone with some kids? Did y'all think about that?!" she fumed throwing her hands up in frustration. Honestly D'Mani hadn't considered that happening but there wasn't a reason to. It wasn't like them niggas were following them around like that. And as far as the women knew, Corey was out of the country and not kidnapped and being held hostage.

"Actually we do. It's no reason for them niggas to chase

y'all asses all the way out there when we all here already. Do that make sense to you?" he was keeping his voice as calm as he could, even though he was already beyond frustrated with the entire situation. Not only was niggas gunning for them and their loved ones, but he was supposed to be handling Cheyanne's remains. With the girls leaving, Imani would miss her mother's services, if he even decided to have any type of service since the only people who would be present would be them. He was under an extreme amount of stress and would have loved if Anastasia just went along with things and made it easier on him. Unfortunately, that wasn't going to happen because her last name was *Holiday* and not a single one of them had any chill, and they definitely hated taking orders. He stood up and pulled her body into his, lifting up her chin with a finger.

"Look, let us handle this. These niggas out here reckless as fuck, they ain't playin' no games. If we constantly worried about what might happen to y'all, our heads ain't gone be in this shit. I'm tryna live a comfortable life with you, not one where we're lookin' over our shoulders every day, worried about what might happen to y'all." It was like they were hitting everybody and he wasn't trying to see who would be next or how severe it might be the next time. So far, they'd been pretty lucky but who was to say that *death* would keep sparing them.

"I guess I can understand that, but I guess I'm mostly just worried that something will happen to you and I won't be here." She pouted and moved deeper into the embrace, burying her face in his chest.

"Woman, I'm solid as fuck ain't shit else gone happen. I can promise you that," he lied quickly, finding it easier without having to look into her eyes. The truth was he didn't know what was going to happen. Him and D'Mari had never dealt with so much collateral damage. Not that anyone that they ever lost was a big deal. Anybody worth keeping around kept themselves out of harm's way. Things were different now; they each had women and children that needed their protection and who they were willing to die for. If it came down to it, he would gladly lay his life down for the lives of his family and that was how he knew they needed to leave. If something happened to Anastasia, Kyler, or Imani, he would be ready to take on any army and he wouldn't think it through; he'd just arm up and go tear some shit down.

"Bet not nothin' else happen." She sniffled and playfully punched him in the chest.

"You swear yo lil ass runnin' shit." He wiped the tears that had managed to slip out of her eyes and grinned, hoping to lighten the mood.

"That's cause I do... now move so I can pack all these damn bags up for me and the kids." She pushed him away, seemingly feeling better about having to go away.

"You sure you don't want my help?" Mani asked even though the last thing he felt like doing was packing some fucking clothes. He hated having to pack and Stasia knew that which was why she gave him a stale face as she opened up the suitcases that lay on their bed.

"You know damn well you don't like to pack." She rolled her eyes at him and he grinned widely.

"You right I was just tryna be nice, but I was hopin' you'd say no."

"Get yo ass outta here!" Stasia laughed loudly and threw a pillow at him that he dodged and ran out of the room.

D'Mani knew that everybody had ducked off to talk privately with their women about the trip, so he didn't think anything of it when he came out and no one was around. He made it downstairs and passed Shirley in the hallway leaving the kitchen with a drink in each hand.

"Hold up Aunt Shirley, why you walkin' around with two drinks?" he stopped her and asked.

"Cause I'm grown as hell for one and for two, if y'all think I'm bouta ride with them slow ass nieces of mine and a bunch of babies without pre-gaming, then you got me fucked up!" she huffed, rolling her eyes.

"It's not gone be that bad--"

"Shiiit you ever been in the car with a bunch of catty ass females AND some kids tah! That whole ride bouta be a hot ass mess! I don't even know how them heffas let y'all talk them into leavin' anyway! Gotta be the dick that got they asses so gone! And pimp dick the worst kind... trust me I know!"

"I ain't a pimp man," D'Mani tried to defend himself. She was really going overboard with that shit.

"Hmph let you tell it. If pimps don't know nothin' else though, they know how to fuck and lie!" she frowned before walking off, talking shit under her breath. All D'Mani could do was shake his head at the old lady. They weren't even on the road yet and he could tell it was going to be an annoying ass ride with their Aunt. It was no wonder all of them were crazy having to grow up with her around.

He continued on his way to find the kids and saw them sitting in the living room watching T.V. D'Mani loved how close Kyler and Imani had gotten in the short time they'd known each other. Kyler was even letting her watch *Sophia the First* and D'Mani knew that was the last thing Kyler wanted to watch, but he sat right next to her like he enjoyed the show too. A smile graced his face as he realized that after everything died down, Imani would be in a stable and loving family with a big brother and stepmom that loved her like he did. He planned on asking to adopt Kyler once him and Stasia finally got married; he knew that would make her happy and it just felt like the right thing to do. Just as he prepared

36

himself to enter the room so that he could talk to them about the trip, his phone chimed. He pulled it out to see a text from Corey's phone. Whoever had him had finally sent in a demand and of course it was some damn money. Before responding, he went in search of D'Mari and J.R. so they could figure out their next move.

8

etween Deana's whining and annoying conversations, Larry trying to get information out of him, and Julian's weak ass threats, Corey was ready to tell them niggas to pull the trigger just to get away from their asses. They had done everything from threatening to rape his wife to chopping his balls off, trying to get him on their team but Corey wasn't budging. He had done enough shit to his family over the months and he'll be damned if he sold them out to any damn body. Especially some clown ass suckers like Julian and Larry, but his lack of cooperation got him fucked up.

After days of abuse, Corey was barely holding on. His eyes were halfway closed and the constant pain that he felt in his body intensified even worse than before. The blood stains on his clothes went from little drops here and there to medium size puddles on his shirt and jeans. If it wasn't for the couple trips he took to the bathroom, his legs probably would've been numb. Although he was losing blood slowly, Corey felt like he could pass out at any minute. He hadn't eaten anything since he'd been captured and the possible lack of food had him feeling faint. The feeling of *defeat* was starting to kick in, but Corey was determined to hold on because he knew for a fact that his brothers were going to rescue him soon.

After his trip to the bathroom, Deana helped Corey wash his hands before retying his legs to the chair. Sitting in the chair in front of him, she went back to feeding him. The chicken from Popeye's along with the red beans and rice was hitting the spot. Even though he was still plotting on how he was going to kill Deana's snake ass, he appreciated her for looking out for him.

"Do you want another piece of chicken?"

"Nah, I'm good," Corey replied, licking the grease off his lips. "Thank you for the food," he spoke dryly.

"You don't sound very appreciative," Deana smacked.

"How can I be under the circumstances?"

Deana didn't answer. She finished cleaning up and threw the trash away before sitting back in the chair. Corey watched her as she examined his bruised face. He knew that something was on her mind but she wasn't expressing it.

"Say what's on your mind Deana?"

She stared at him a moment longer before responding.

"I just don't understand why you're going through all this torture and pain for niggas that probably aren't even looking for you. Why don't you just save yourself, join Julian and Larry, and be on your way?" Deana suggested in a sweet tone.

By the statement she'd just made, Corey instantly saw through their plan and couldn't help the chuckle that escaped his lips.

"Let me explain something to you, ma. *Them* niggas you're referring to ain't no niggas I just met. They're *my fucking family* and despite what you may believe, they are looking for me and for the fact that you just tried to *First Forty-eight* me is real cute Deana."

39

"What are you talking about Corey?"

"Come on, man. You gonna come down here feeding me fucking Popeye's and shit, then suggest that I turn on my folks and link up with these clown ass niggas to save my own ass when there is still a possibility that they might kill my ass if I did decide to switch sides. You coulda brought an Ultimate Feast in here from *Red Lobster* to try to get me to change my mind and my answer wouldn't have change. I'm not giving them motherfuckas shit! Instead of fucking me up, they need to just kill me because they ain't got no use for me."

"These niggas really think you stupid. I told them dumb motherfuckas that you were gonna see through that shit," she shook her head. "Well at least I tried."

Corey shook his head at the fact that Julian and Larry thought their plan would work. The more they tried to insult his intelligence, the more offended he became. They say to *never* underestimate your opponent and they were trying to play him for *sweet*. Instead of being angry, Corey just laughed it off. Moments later, the front door opened, and Deana went upstairs. He could hear her cussing them out for being stupid and not coming up with a better plan. He tried to listen to the rest of their conversation, but their voices drifted off as they moved to another part of the house. A few minutes later, the clowns came in the basement grinning from ear to ear.

"I gotta hand it to youngin'. I didn't think you'd be able to hold out this long. Most young niggas turn into running faucets when they're under pressure but you didn't fold. You continue to amaze me," Larry patted his back. "I just want you know that I'll be getting what I want soon enough."

"And what's that?"

"Money, murder, and revenge. After using your phone to get in contact with your people, I sent them a ransom message letting them know how much I wanted. When they agree to bring the money, we'll kill your squad, take the money, then take out the Tessa Cartel, and I'll be back in my rightful place once and for all," Larry smirked, staring off into space.

"But what if they don't text us back O.G?"

"Trust me. They'll text back."

"I'm just ready to kill this nigga. I'm tired of all this waiting!" Julian pulled out his gun, placing it to Corey's head.

"Julian cool the fuck out!" Larry pulled him away from Corey. "I don't know if you jealous of this nigga or what but you need to keep your fucking emotions in check!"

"My nut ass cousin brought me as a *backup* for this cornball ass nigga when I shoulda been a part of the original lineup! I'm nobodies fucking back up! That nigga got me chopped!"

"You shoulda handled that shit when he first asked you. You agreed to be apart of the team and you didn't want to play ball. So, *you* set your cousin up and went into hiding. I'm trying to protect your ass, but if you can't stick to the fucking plan, then I'm a get rid of your bitch ass and do this take over shit myself. Now, if and when I want this nigga dead, I'll give you the word but until then, *don't* pull that fucking gun out again."

Corey watched the showdown between the two men as if he was watching a movie. He was intrigued by Julian's reason as to why he was ready to kill him and why he set up J.R. and although he though his reason was some fuck boy shit, he understood. Corey felt some type of way when Mari told him that they brought another nigga into the operation to help out with the day to day. He felt like he was being replaced but learned to deal with it because it was something that needed to get done to keep shit moving smoothly; but no one figured that J.R.'s family would do him dirty like that.

After they calmed down, Julian tucked his gun back in his waistband and took off up the stairs. Corey chuckled to himself because Julian was always quick to call him a *bitch ass nigga* when *he* was *the real bitch*. Larry took a seat in one of the chairs and was glued to his phone. Minutes later, the familiar text tone played on Corey's phone and his eyes grew wide. Larry checked the message and a smile appeared on his face.

"They agreed to give me the money I asked for. Now all I have to do is give them the time and the meeting place."

Corey's jaws tighten at the thought of his brothers giving them money just to get them back; but being as though he knew them all too well, Larry's ass wasn't going to see one dime of that money or live to see another day.

9

Anastasia and her sisters were up bright and early ready to care of business, but of course their Aunt Shirley was still on the let out bed snoring and sleeping off all the liquor she'd drunk the night before. The sisters had tried to wake her up at least three times each, but she was not budging and Stasia was already over it.

"Man let's just leave her ass y'all, she ain't bouta wake up," she huffed, folding her arms across her chest.

"Hell naw! We not leavin' my favorite Aunty! Who Ima smoke with if she don't go?" Lexi was already shaking her head in disagreement.

"Well then you can stay here with her and y'all can smoke all y'all want whenever she wakes up!"

"Bitch don't play with me, you know I ain't missin' this action!" Lexi snapped, rolling her eyes at Anastasia.

"Come on then. You gone be fine hell, we bout ain't gone even have enough time for you to smoke anyway." Drea pulled her purse up on her shoulder with a shrug.

"Yeah let's just go y'all cause I'm startin' to get anxious," Lyssa said as she shuffled from one foot to the other.

"You better shake that shit off, cause if we come up on that Deana hoe, you can't be soundin' like no weak ass bitch!"

"Lexi yo ass sound just like Shirley," Stasia sighed. Her baby sister and their Aunt had been spending way too much time together, to the point where Lexi was starting to sound like a little mini Shirley or maybe she had already been sounding that way.

"Thank you bitch,." Lexi smirked and winked in her sister's direction.

"Girl you know that wasn't no compliment."

"It was to me." Of course Lexi was completely unfazed by the insult because Shirley was her fave.

"Ayite we ain't got time for this. We already damn near an hour late since we been in here messin' with Shirley and y'all heffas goin' back and forth."

"Okay, let's go then,." Lexi said quickly. Drea looked at the Stasia and Alyssa with her brow raised.

"Shit I been ready to go.," Anastasia shrugged and picked up her purse and the keys.

"Well what y'all hoes waitin' on?" Drea quipped, opening the door.

THE SISTERS PULLED UP TO THE REHABILITATION CENTER fanning smoke out of their faces since Lexi had insisted on smoking. Anastasia was surprised that Lexi was able to finish two blunts before they'd gotten there and she was sure that she had a contact high just from how loud the weed was. Her sister was definitely making up for not smoking while pregnant and the time she'd been breastfeeding.

"Okay so what we gonna say when we get in here?" Lexie asked, leaning into the front seat between Stasia and Drea.

"Shit I don't know. It's Alyssa's husband so she could just say that she hasn't heard from him and wanted to know if he'd checked himself back in." They all nodded and agreed that that sounded like a good idea before getting out and walking inside. As soon as they entered, they noticed patients of the facility sitting around or walking in a zombie like state.

"Biiiitch these people up in here look like they just stepped out the crack house," Lexi whispered loudly, looking around with wide eyes.

"Could you be any louder Alexis?" Drea hissed back, trying hard not to laugh.

"They asses don't hear nothin' but the monkey on they back!"

That time, Drea, Stasia, or Lyssa couldn't hold back and they all erupted in laughter. That was when Anastasia knew that she had definitely caught a contact right along with her sisters. Their laughing seized when they reached the desk where an elderly black lady sat giving them the eye.

"Gone head bitch," Lexi said, pushing Alyssa forward.

"How may I help you?" the lady asked sharply, staring at them over the top of her thick glasses.

"Ummmm... yes. My husband Corey Washington recently checked himself out of here, and I haven't been able to reach him, so I was wondering if maybe he had come back?" Lyssa's voice cracked a little as she spoke. Anastasia rubbed her back, worried that she might start crying again before they even got any answers.

"Hump! Well I can just check the system right here and let you know, but I doubt if he's back." She pushed her glasses back up her nose and started to type on the computer in front of her.

"What makes you say that?" Drea asked with a hand on her hip.

"Because usually when people leave here and go missing, they've relapsed. Honestly, he's probably somewhere getting high and you should be making a police report instead of coming here looking."

"Oh hell naw! Bitch I wil...." Lexi started to reach over the desk but Drea held her back.

"Ma'am, I'm Mrs. Washington's attorney and I would advise that you refrain from *ever* making personal opinions to the family of patients in this facility or I'll have you fired faster than you can say unemployment," Drea sneered and slapped her hand on the desk in irritation. "Now do what she asked thank you." The lady went back to typing, clearly flustered since Drea had put the pressure on her. After a few minutes, she looked back at them as if she had bad news.

"He's not in our system as being checked back in."

"Okay well he was close to a nurse here named Deana. Is she here? Can we talk to her?" Anastasia pressed.

"Yeah where that Deana bitch at?" Lexi came from behind Drea and asked loudly, causing Drea to pinch the bridge of her nose.

"Umm Deana?" The lady nervously said looking around. "There she is."

Alyssa followed her gaze and caught sight of a woman stopping in the middle of the hall and then taking off when their eyes met.

"There she go!" She shouted to her sisters and took off behind her. Deana ran through the hallway like she was avoiding the police as Alyssa and Lexi went after her.

"I'm bouta get the truck," Stasia told Drea who was starting to go after them. Anastasia hustled to the vehicle, glad that she had decided to leave it parked in the fire lane instead of parking. She raced around the side of the building in the direction that her sisters had gone in just enough time to see a dark car speeding out of the lot. A second later, Drea, Lexi, and Lyssa came out of the back exit looking around as they tried to catch their breaths.

Beeping the horn, Stasia stopped the truck in front of them.

"Hurry up y'all... she just pulled off!" She shouted and they all jumped in and she cut the wheel, speeding out of the parking lot and hitting a right in hopes of catching up to Deana. "That's the car right there y'all." She pointed out the car that she'd seen the girl leave in at the light a couple of cars ahead of them.

"Okay stay on her Stasia but don't let her see you."

"Yeah that bitch might lead us to Corey, cause her ass ran up outta there too fast to be innocent," Lexi added.

"Y'all really think that he would have the guys lie for him so he could be here playin' house with this bitch?" Alyssa questioned and Anastasia looked at her through the rear view. She didn't want to assume anything, but like Lexi had said, Deana running like that was suspect as hell.

"We not gone jump to conclusions y'all," Drea said calmly, finally having returned her breathing to normal.

"Well she need her ass beat for makin' me run anyway so I'm lookin' for any excuse," Lexi smacked her lips.

"Look she slowing down. She bouta turn!" Drea said, pointing and Anastasia followed suit, turning onto the same street where Deana pulled her car over. Staying a few houses away, Stasia parked and cut the lights off as the sisters watched Deana exit her car and damn near run up on the porch, looking around on some paranoid shit. She knocked instead of walking right in. Surprised that she hadn't gone home, the sisters all watched closely to see who would open the door. When it was swung open, they each breathed a sigh of relief that it wasn't Corey, even though it was a man.

"Oh my god y'all! I was bouta have a heart attack if Corey had opened that door!" Alyssa gasped.

"And I was bouta catch another case!" Lexi chimed proudly.

"Girrrl..." Drea rolled her eyes and laughed. The mood was a little bit lighter since they hadn't caught Corey doing dirt, but they still knew something wasn't right about that whole Deana situation.

"Oh shit! Aunty Shirley FaceTiming me y'all!"

Anastasia still had her eyes glued to the two people on the porch talking and looking around before they finally went inside. That shit was weird as hell and instead of clearing Deana's name, it only made her more suspicious.

"Don't answer that shit!" Drea warned but Lexi had already connected the call.

"Heeey favorite Aunty!"

"Bitch don't favorite Aunty me! Why y'all leave me?"

"We tried to wake you up--"

"Well y'all ain't try hard enough! I told you if I'm sleep and don't wake up to put a lil wake and bake under my nose or crack open a bottle of *Crown Royal* and dap it on my lip! I'll jump up like them people in the coffee commercials!" she shouted, making the truck erupt into loud laughter. "Y'all laughin' and I'm serious!"

"We bouta be on our way back anyway Aunty... we gotta regroup," Drea tossed over her shoulder, motioning for Stasia to pull off. They'd already committed the address to memory and just in case, Stasia had taken a picture of the house with her phone and locked in the location too.

"You okay Lyssa?" Stasia asked, looking at her in the rear view mirror for the hundredth time.

"Yeah I'm just tryna figure out if I'm relieved or disappointed that we didn't find him," she answered quietly, looking out of the window at the cars whipping by on their way home.

"Well I think you should count it as a blessing... at least we ain't catch him on some shady shit," Drea said and Anastasia nodded in agreement. "Let's go get us something to drink and then we'll go back to the room and put our heads together about our next move."

"I agree about the drink!" Shirley chimed in still on the phone with Lexi. Anastasia shook her head but started in the direction of the nearest liquor store so that they could go and get their plan together.

❦ 10 ❦

"So y'all really *not* gon' say shit to me this entire ride?" J.R. asked, looking over at Lexi who was in the passenger's seat before looking in the rearview mirror at Aunt Shirley and Lyssa.

"Y'ALL HEAR SUM? CUZ I DON'T," LEXI REPLIED BEFORE shifting in her seat.

SHE HAD HEARD J.R. LOUD AND CLEAR THIS TIME AND THE other nine hundred times he had spoken, but it didn't stop her from ignoring him. As a matter of fact, the five-hour drive to Mississippi was actually easier than she thought it would be. Although Stasia and Drea were riding in another truck, their Holiday Sisters' group chat was lit with jokes and gifs about the guys.

"I KNOW YOU DON'T WANT TO LEAVE BUT LEXI, YOU HAVE

no choice. I don't know why I gotta keep saying the shit," J.R. growled as he turned into the driveway of her childhood home.

"YOU *THE ONLY* MOTHERFUCKER TALKING," SHE SNAPPED, shooting him a look before reaching for the door handle.

BEFORE LEXI KNEW IT, HER LOWER BODY WAS OUT OF THE car while her upper half was now in the driver's seat.

"YOU *BETTER* WATCH WHO THE FUCK YOU TALKING TO," J.R. growled inside her ear.

"NO.... *YOU* BETTER LET GO OF MY MOTHERFUCK'N' PONYTAIL!" she yelled, swinging wildly over her head in his direction.

J.R. AND LEXI TUSSLED BRIEFLY UNTIL A TIRED LEXI GAVE up, allowing him to pin her down.

"I LOVE YOU SHORTY," HE TOWERED OVER HER AND SAID, staring into her eyes.

LEXI LOOKED UP AT HIM AND THROUGH CLINCHED TEETH she mouthed, "Let me go bro."

J.R. QUICKLY STOLE A KISS BEFORE GETTING OUT THE CAR. Lexi too jumped out after grabbing her purse. She fixed her clothes and her hair, just as the other truck pulled up. Lyssa and Shirley took the babies inside while J.R.'s tall skinny ass struggled with the bags. The thought of helping him crossed her mind but she quickly dismissed that idea. Instead, she grabbed her phone to text her homie so he could call his weed man. If Lexi was going to be away from her man and in a house with her sisters, plus those crying ass babies, she needed at least a pound.

"WHAT YOU DOING AND WHY YO HAIR LIKE THAT?" DREA appeared over her shoulder and questioned, trying to read her messages.

"DAMN.... BUT IF YOU MUST KNOW, I'M TRYING TO GET me some weed," she replied honestly.

"WEEEEEDDDD? LEXI, AREN'T YOU BREASTFEEDING?"

"YES, I WAS BUT AMIR IS ALMOST TWO MONTHS. I THINK he'll be aight," she explained.

"GIRL THAT DON'T MAKE NO DAMN SENSE. COME ON," SHE giggled.

DREA GRABBED LEXI BY THE ARM AND PULLED HER IN THE

house. She knew how Drea liked to lecture, so she considered herself getting off easy; therefore, she just went with the flow.

Once inside, everyone reunited with their mom Victoria and her friend who cooked up a feast for the crew. Lexi purposely didn't eat the ride to Mississippi so she could pig out once she got there. Victoria was undoubtedly one of the best cooks in Jackson and everyone knew it.

"Y'ALL WANNA GO GET WASHED UP SO Y'ALL CAN EAT?" Victoria stated, stirring the mixed greens in the pot that sat on the stove.

"ACTUALLY MA, WE ABOUT TO HEAD RIGHT OUT. WE GOTTA get those trucks back before....." J.R. started but was cut off by Lexi.

"LET ME HOLLER AT YOU," SHE SAID UNDER HER BREATH, pulling him by the hand towards the door.

LEXI USHERED J.R. ONTO THE PORCH AND ONCE THE FRONT door closed behind them, she let him have it.

"ARE YOU FUCK'N' SERIOUS?" SHE SNAPPED, MOVING AND gesturing with her hands in his face.

"GIRL GONE," HE STEPPED BACK, SWATTING AT HER LIKE AN annoying house fly.

"No, I'm for real. Y'all not going to spend time with us before y'all disappear and do God knows what in Atlanta?" she asked, twisting her head to the side.

Lexi could tell by J.R.'s demeanor that she was starting to piss him off but she didn't care. She never ever bitched at him on a regular, but something about this little separation was really eating at her.

"Look. The quicker I leave, the sooner I'll be back. Relax. I'm going to call y'all every hour baby. I need you to trust me," he said, pleading with his eyes.

Lexi knew her husband was being sincere and trusting him was the best thing to do but some shit was easier said than done.

"Ok, I'm going to trust you BUT I need you to come back to me in one piece," she smiled.

"I got you."

"Aight, go ahead before I change my mind," she said, pushing him back in the house.

"Aye. I do got time for some head though," he stopped in his tracks before turning around and whispering.

LEXI LET OUT A LOUD LAUGH BEFORE JOINING EVERYONE back in the kitchen. Each Holiday sister said their goodbyes to their men before they sat down and ate. During dinner, Lexi couldn't help but wonder and worry about J.R. She hoped putting all her trust in him wasn't going to come back and bite her in the ass.

THE SISTERS ALL DECIDED TO PUT THE KIDS DOWN FOR NAPS after they ate. Sleeping in her old room brought back so many memories, both good and bad. Nothing had changed about the bedroom décor except the teddy bears she use to sleep with was now replaced by her own child.

Lexi rubbed Amir's soft chubby hand as he stirred in his sleep. The one time he slept through the night, she couldn't even dose off to take advantage. Checking her phone for the hundredth time, Lexi snatched it off the charger, propped a few pillows up to block Amir, and headed out the room.

She slowly tip-toed down the hallway towards the stairs when she heard noise coming from Alyssa's room. Lexi stood still and listened a little closer, realizing she was crying. Not thinking twice, she knocked one time, just for warning and entered.

"MY BAD. I THOUGHT EVERYONE WAS SLEEP," SHE QUICKLY sat up and wiped the tears from her eyes.

"YOU GOOD? WHY YOU CRYING?" LEXI ASKED, WALKING deeper in the room.

"GIRL, I'M GOOD," LYSSA REPLIED, LETTING OUT A fake laugh.

"NAH, THAT'S SOME BULLSHIT. I'LL BE BACK."

LEXI STORMED OUT OF THE ROOM AND DOWN THE HALL TO where Drea slept. She woke her up cautiously, so she wouldn't disturb the twins. After pulling her out the room, they went and did the same with Stasia. Once everyone was up, they headed back to Alyssa.

"NOW TELL THE TRUTH BEFORE WE BEAT YO ASS. WHY YOU crying?" Lexi asked, flipping on the light.

"ALEXIS, CALM DOWN..... LYSSA, WHAT'S WRONG?" DREA asked calmly while Stasia rolled her eyes at Lexi.

"IT'S COREY. I'M SCARED Y'ALL, IT'S BEEN *TOO* MANY DAYS," she cried into her hands.

ALL THREE SISTERS HUDDLED AROUND AND CONSOLED HER, giving the best advice they could think of. Lexi wouldn't know how to act if it was J.R. that had disappeared. She felt bad for her sister but sitting there crying miles away wasn't gon' solve shit.

"AYE, Y'ALL REMEMBER THAT BOOK WE READ WHERE THREE

56

men came up missing and their wives painted the city red looking for them?" Lexi asked out the blue.

"YEAAAAHHHHH. WHY?" STASIA SIDE EYED HER and asked.

"LET'S DO THAT. LOOK, WE SMARTER THAN THOSE NIGGAS. I'm willing to bet that's the reason they sent us off," Lexi replied.

"BUT WHAT IF COREY REALLY IS AWAY ON BUSINESS?" Alyssa poor naïve heart asked.

"BUT WHAT IF HE NOT?" LEXI SHOT BACK.

"BUT LEXI... THEN WHAT? WE AIN'T NO HOOD WIVES AND this ain't no book," Drea added in.

"LISTEN, I AIN'T SAYING LET'S GO GET AK'S AND NINES AND shoot shit up. All I'm saying is, let's stop being scary and step up."

"STEP UP? GIRL WE ARE DAUGHTERS OF A PREACHER. YOU need to put those Urban Fiction books down," Stasia chuckled.

ALYSSA AND DREA LAUGHED ALONG WITH HER WHILE LEXI stood there quiet.

"OH WAIT... SHE'S SERIOUS!" DREA STOPPED LAUGHING AND zoomed in closer to Lexi.

"I'M DEAD ASS. I AIN'T SAYING BE RIDERS, BUT I BEEN *THE bitch of a dope boy* long enough to know how this shit go," Lexi explained.

SILENCE FELL AMONGST THE ROOM WHILE EVERYONE STARED at each other with perplexed looks on their face.

"FINDING MY SISTER CRYING IN THE DARK AIN'T SITTING right with me, so what y'all wanna do?" Lexi asked, searching each of their faces for a clue.

"I'M DOWN," DREA SAID FIRST FOLLOWED BY STASIA.

EACH SISTER LOOKED AT LYSSA WHO STOOD UP, "LET'S GO find my husband."

"BACK TO A-T-L WE GO THEN......"

11

"Are y'all sure we need to do this? I really don't wanna leave my baby," Lyssa whined as the sisters got comfortable in the Suburban.

"Bitch... we goin' to see what's up wit *YO HUSBAND!!*" Lexi quipped.

"I know Lexi... don't start yo shit. I just know I'm gonna be missing my baby and you got a baby too," Lyssa fired back.

"Y'all chill out. We all got kids. Mama and Ms. Linda will be fine with the kids. Kyler and Imani will be a big help and not to mention... Aunt Shirley can help too," Drea chimed in to diffuse the situation.

After she said added her two cents, Drea turned around and got comfortable in the passenger's seat while Stasia was at the wheel. She prayed that Lexi and Lyssa would be okay in the back.

"Y'all hoes ready?" Stasia quizzed after putting her phone in the cup holder.

"Yeah, biggest hoe," Lexi replied.

"I'll be glad when J.R. knock yo ass up again. You was

nicer when you was pregnant," Stasia retorted and put the truck in gear.

Right before she could pull away, the door was snatched open and they all screamed and jumped.

"Y'all heifers ain't leaving me wit a house full of *Bebe's kids*. Fuck that!" Aunt Shirley declared.

"Auntie you can't go wit us. We on a mission," Drea explained.

"I heard y'all plotting. I ain't gon' get in the way... plus Victoria and Linda got them damn kids. We all need this break from 'em," Aunt Shirley insisted, and Drea bit her tongue to keep from saying what she was thinking.

"My favorite auntie can go. She ain't gon' be in the way," Lexi chimed in.

"You just want her to go so y'all asses can smoke," Drea rolled her eyes and Lexi flipped her off.

"Thank you favorite niece... besides, if I don't go, I'll call y'all men and tell them to be on the lookout for y'all wanna be inspector gadget looking asses," Aunt Shirley hopped on in with her bag.

"Snitching ass," Stasia mumbled and pulled away after everyone was ready.

"Okay we should arrive around midnight. I'll book us a room at the Courtyard by Marriott" Drea said as she typed away on her phone.

"How many nights we gon' need?" Lyssa asked.

"I have no idea, but I'll book two just in case," Drea replied as she confirmed the reservation.

"Sisters, once all of this is handled, it's time for another trip. We haven't been anywhere in a whole year," Drea suggested.

"Oooh I'm in," Aunt Shirley answered before either of the sisters could and they all laughed.

"She said *sisters*," Stasia mumbled, but Aunt Shirley heard her.

"At least I wasn't *a sister wife*," Aunt Shirley fired back.

"Keep on Auntie and Ima turn around and take you back home with mama," Stasia hit the brakes.

"Okay okay Ima be good... come on Lexi, fire that shit up."

"Y'all ain't smoking in here," Drea turned around in her seat.

"We can either smoke in here or y'all gon' have to stop and let us smoke. Choice is yours, but we gon' smoke," Lexi offered.

"You two make me sick," Drea rolled her eyes at turned back around.

"You need this contact anyway... loosen up."

Drea ignored her and hit the email application on her phone. Even though she had taken a leave from the office, she was still handling business via email. She saw the reply to an email that she had been waiting on and clicked on it first. Drea was really hesitant to reach out at first, but Mari told her to contact the best for J.R., so she did just that. Even though they had a rough patch in the past, he was still good at what he did. She replied to the email and was confident that the outcome would be great as long as D'Mari held up to his end of the bargain.

"Baby boy, your love, got me trippin' on you... you know your love is big enough, make me trip up on you."

Lexi's loud, off key singing ass made Drea laugh out loud. The rest of the sister joined in with their sister and sang the next few songs to the top of their lungs. Before they knew it, Stasia had reached the halfway mark and took the next exit so they could get some gas and a few snacks. Right when she pulled up to the pump, Drea's phone rang and her heart sank when she noticed that it was a FaceTime call from her husband.

"Oh shit... I didn't think he was gonna FaceTime tonight," she stated nervously.

"You better act normal and answer," Lexi suggested.

Drea slid the bar across and got out of the truck.

"Hey babe," she smiled.

"Hey love... damn where you at?" Mari wasted no time asking.

"We came to the store to grab some snacks. What you doin'?" she asked.

"Discussing some shit wit the fellas. I wanted to see the kids before they tapped out."

"Well you already missed 'em babe. I guess the drive this morning wore them out. I miss you though."

"I miss you too. We'll all be together again soon," Mari promised.

"I know babe. I'll be sure you see the kids on FaceTime tomorrow."

"Bet. I love you."

"I love you more," Drea ended the call.

She was glad that her mom had an iPhone, so she didn't lie to her husband. She hoped they could all keep their lies straight while on their little mission or they were gonna be screwed.

After gassing up and grabbing snacks, Drea was prepared to drive, but Stasia hopped back in the driver's seat and she didn't complain at all. Once they were back on Interstate 20, Drea learned that all of the men had called at the same time. That only let her know that they were up to no good just like them.

The girls arrived at the hotel twenty minutes after eleven, thanks to Stasia's fast driving ass. They checked into their suite and got settled. Aunt Shirley got the let out couch while Drea and Lexi and Lyssa and Stasia shared beds.

"So y'all we done talked shit the whole way about everything except why we here... sooo what's our plan for tomorrow?" Stasia queried.

"Yeah we gotta figure it out cuz these niggaz are lying. Lyssa, you sure you ain't run the man off?" Lexi quizzed and Lyssa looked like she wanted to slap her ass.

"Lyssa, what y'all done had goin' on tho for real? Anything you haven't told us?" Drea asked.

While she was waiting on an answer, Drea went to her text messages and forwarded the pictures of the twins that her mom sent to Mari.

"Well... we did have an argument about a bitch name Deana that worked at the rehab. He said she was doing shit for him because he didn't wanna bother me, but my husband wouldn't leave me like that," Alyssa defended Corey.

"Wellllll... he is missing and his phone goin' straight to voicemail, so we gotta take everything into consideration sis," Drea replied and Alyssa broke down and started crying. Everyone huddled around Alyssa and comforted her.

"It's gonna be okay Lyssa boo," Drea said.

"Lyssa you know we gon' beat that bitch ass... stop crying," Lexi advised.

"Yeah Lyssa, we got you," Stasia chimed in.

"I'll swing my purse on that ol' heifer too, but you might wanna let her have the crackhead and get you a new man," Aunt Shirley walked out of the bathroom and said.

Everyone laughed at that comment and it lightened the mood. The sisters, along with their aunt, conversed about everything that had been going on and continued putting their heads together. The guys never gave them any details surrounding their 'businesses', but they were all smart. The

Holiday Sisters were smart enough to stay out of the way, but smart enough to know what was going on. However, it was time to step in and help their men out. They all went to bed with their minds on going to the rehab the next morning and finding that bitch named Deana that had been texting Corey.

12

After picking up some *Henny*, *Crown Royal,* and *1800 Margarita*, the sisters went back to the hotel room to get lit. Aunt Shirley gave the sisters an earful until she saw the bottles of liquor; she filled her flask before grabbing a cup, filling it up to the brim. In need of ice, Anastasia left the room with the bucket, re-entering the room seconds later. Once the sisters had their cups filled, they sat down and filled their Aunt in on the day's event.

"What the fuck you mean that bitch got away? How y'all let that hoe out run y'all?" Aunt Shirley interrupted Lexi who was giving her the run down.

"If you wouldn't have cut Lexi off, you woulda found out that we followed the bitch to some house and the nigga that answered the door wasn't Corey," Stasia shook her head.

"But even though Corey didn't answer the door, we still think that bitch Deana is a suspect," Lyssa sipped her drink.

"Yeah, that bitch definitely knows something," Drea chimed.

Aunt Shirley was about to speak but the sisters cut her off.

"Yes we got the address."

"Good because y'all hoes can act slow sometimes," Aunt Shirley took her cup to the head. "So, we got a suspicious bitch, an address, and no crackhead. I don't know y'all. Maybe them niggas are tellin' the truth. Maybe he did take a trip."

"If that's the case, then why did they ship us off to Mississippi? And if his ass was taking a trip some damn where, why the fuck wouldn't my husband tell me?" Alyssa fought back tears. "Nah. Something is wrong. My nigga wouldn't just up and leave like that."

The room fell silent as the ladies sat deep in thought. Alyssa downed her first cup and poured herself another. This mission to find Corey had her nerves all out of sorts and she was ready for their search to be over. Although she was anxious to find her husband, her fear of learning that he was up to no good was Alyssa's main concern; but so far, that wasn't the case. Thinking back to how Deana took off running when she saw them, Alyssa couldn't help but to wonder why she ran. Normally, if a nigga's wife came looking for the other woman, she'd be ready to tell the wife any and everything. No matter if it was true or not but Deana didn't do that. The only time motherfuckers run is when they got something to hide.

"Oh my God!" Alyssa shouted, startling everyone.

"What the fuck Lyssa? You almost made me spill my drink!" Lexi shouted.

"What if Corey was inside the house?"

They all looked at each other with wide eyes.

"That could be possible but why would he be in the house?" Stasia questioned.

"I don't know but something is definitely off with shawty. Either he's in that house or that bitch knows where he is."

"That bitch Deana might know where he is, but I don't think he's in the house, Lyssa," Drea down her second cup.

"What if he's being held captive?"

"Held captive? Why the hell would anyone hold the crackhead hostage?" Aunt Shirley caused the sisters to laugh.

"Lyssa, I think you're over thinking things," Stasia shook her head. "Look, they said that he went out of town on trip. How about we try to locate his passport and if we find it, then we can start thinking the worse, aight?"

Alyssa nodded her head in agreement. Trying to free her mind of any negative thoughts of Corey, the nagging feeling in her stomach was telling her not to. She didn't know if it was her woman's intuition of knowing that Corey was some-where in Georgia but whatever it was wouldn't allow Alyssa to believe otherwise.

After drinking until one in the morning, the sisters woke up around nine the next morning due to Aunt Shirley's alarm going off. While the sisters got dressed, their phone seemed to ring one after the other with calls from their men. Alyssa laughed as she listened to the lies they told them when they asked to see the kids and where they were. As much as she tried to stay strong, she found herself missing her husband more and more with each passing day. Every time Alyssa thought about the last time she saw him, she regretted sending him to the store. Besides all of the negative thoughts that were running through her mind, Alyssa was positive that they would find her husband. The only thing she was unsure of was if Corey was going to be found dead or alive.

When everyone was ready, they left out of the hotel making their way to their truck. Slamming the doors shut, Anastasia cranked the engine before pulling out of the spot.

"Ummm, where exactly am I going, Lyssa?"

"We gotta go to my crib so I can see if his passport is there."

"You mean the mansion?" Lexi questioned.

"Nooo. My house house."

"Well before we go there, we need to stop and get something to eat," Aunt Shirley stated.

"Can't you eat after we come from my house? It ain't gonna take me that long to find what I'm looking for," Lyssa turned to look at her aunt.

"Look heffa, it ain't gonna matter if you find that passport now or in the next twenty minutes. That crackhead husband of your is still gonna be missing. That shit can wait. My stomach pains can't. Now take me to *Wendy's* or something so I can get some damn food."

Alyssa turned back around in her seat and checked the messages that came through on her phone. Her mother sent her a few pictures of their daughter to her phone and it instantly brought a smile to her face. Between Corey missing and being away from her baby, Alyssa didn't know who she missed more, but she couldn't wait until they were all back together again.

Pulling into the first *Wendy's* they saw, Anastasia got in the long drive thru line.

"Not uh. This line is too fucking long. Park the car and let me out."

Letting out a sigh of frustration, Anastasia did what she was told then popped the locks for them to get out. Aunt Shirley hopped out the car and Lexi followed suit.

"Y'all hoes want something?" Lexi shouted.

"Get me a Strawberry Lemonade and some baconator fries," Drea replied.

Alyssa shook her head as she continued to focus on her phone. She went to Corey's text thread and read the last text messages they sent to each other. She smiled as she read the messages of him expressing his love to her. Her eyes began to water but she dabbed them quickly with her sleeves before the tears could fall.

"Oh shit! Y'all get down!" Drea ducked down in the back seat.

On que, Lyssa and Stasia slid in their seats.

"What the fuck are we ducking for Drea?" Lyssa questioned

"I just saw the twins go inside the *Wendy's*!"

"You fucking lyin'!" Stasia shouted.

Minutes later, they heard Lexi and Aunt Shirley sounding like they were ready to fight. Looking up to see what was going on, they saw Lexi arguing with the twins. When they saw J.R emerge from the car, the sisters hopped out the truck and jogged over to where the commotion was at. Joining in on the argument, everyone was talking all at once so no one person understood the other.

"Everybody shut the fuck for a minute!" Aunt Shirley yelled, getting everyone's attention. "I understand that everyone is angry but we're not gonna do this shit in public. Everybody get in their cars and meet back at the mansion."

Both groups headed towards their cars and hopped in. Trying to get their lie together, Alyssa told them that she would take the rap for this, but no one was going to let her take the fall alone.

❧ 13 ❧

"First of all, you gon' stop hollering at me like I'm your child!" Lexi hissed as she folded her arms across her chest.

J.R. took both hands and massaged his temples as he tried to process everything.

"All I wanted was a four for four," he stated, shaking his head.

"Me too nephew," Aunt Shirley chimed in from the couch.

"*Me too nephew?*" Stasia repeated, twisting her lips to the side, mimicking her aunt.

"It's all yo fault, had you not made us stop...." Drea added in but was cut off by Shirley fanning her hand around in the air.

"Y'all not gon' blame me, y'all better blame Lexi. If it wasn't for her getting me that high, I wouldn't even have the munchies," she replied.

"ME?!" Lexi jumped up and yell.

"You know what fav, you right, I shouldn't blame you. I blame Alyssa," Shirley shouted, pointing her skinny wrinkled finger in the direction of Lyssa.

"How is any of this my fault?" Lyssa snapped out of her daze and asked.

"Had you not married a crackhead, we wouldn't be in Atlanta running in dope houses, looking for him, "Shirley explained

"WHO THE FUCK RUNNING IN DOPE HOUSES?" the bass in J.R.'s voice caused everyone to dart eyes in his direction.

"Well technically, we not even sure it is a dope house, we just think Corey is in there doing dope," Lexi explained.

"LEXI!" all three of her sisters shouted her name in unison.

"What?" she shrugged, looking around at them.

J.R. listened as everyone held their own side conversations. He couldn't believe the Holiday Sisters had the audacity to bring their asses back to Atlanta after they explained to them how important it was for them to be in Mississippi. He knew the women were hardheaded and head strong, but he never expected them to do no shit like that.

"Aye... aye.... Aye... everybody needs to chill. The fact that y'all so smart but don't fucking think is killing me," D'Mani chimed in.

"Exactly. Y'all think this shit a game?" D'Mari asked, looking around at each sister.

"Yeah.... They silly ass must think it is," J.R. added in.

"Ok, y'all need to chill. We were only trying to help," Stasia spoke, standing to her feet.

"Help? How the fuck y'all gon' help?" D'Mani turned to her and asked.

The guys waited for an answer but neither girl spoke up; instead they took turns looking at each of the men.

"That's what I thought. Y'all might as well pack y'all shit and get back on the road," D'Mani urged.

"No baby, we came to help and that's what we gon do,"

Drea spoke softly while she rubbed her husband's hand, trying to diffuse the situation.

"Look, I'll take full blame. They were only trying to help me. I miss my husband and I'm worried. I know y'all said he was away on business...."

"BULLSHIT!" Aunt Shirley said, cutting her off with a fake cough.

Everyone in the room eyes darted to her as she tried to play it off by looking in her phone.

"Anyway.... Like I was saying..... Either Corey is cheating or in danger, either way, as his wife, I need answers," Lyssa continued.

J.R. understood that she was worried; any wife in their right mind would be but telling them the truth would be telling too much and they needed to protect their innocence as long as possible.

"We hear y'all but y'all need to hear us and take y'all asses back to Mississippi," D'Mani spoke.

"Ok, we will but I need to ask y'all one question and for the first time, could at least one of y'all be honest with me?" Alyssa pleaded.

"Honest? Tuh..." Lexi smirked but the look J.R. gave her made her remain quiet.

"I really don't expect y'all to trick on y'all brother, but I just need to know if it's another woman?" Lyssa asked.

"Another woman?" J.R. repeated.

"Hell nah sis, you good. Corey loves you. He wouldn't cheat on you," D'Mari assured her.

"But didn't he cheat on her like a year or two ago?" Shirley blurted out, bringing up unwanted memories.

"Auntie chill..." Lexi chuckled, tossing her the flask she made Lexi carry in her purse.

Shirley wasted no time, twisting off the top and taking a swig. They weren't sure how long the *Jamison* was going to shut her up, they just prayed it was long enough for them to get to the bottom of things.

"It's funny y'all say that because, we paid the rehab a visit and when I asked about one of their workers, Deanna, she took off running like she knew something," Lyssa continued once the living room was quiet again.

The name Deanna sounded so familiar. In fact, J.R. remembered exactly where he heard the name from. Corey told them about some crazy ass bitch who worked at the center. According to Corey, she had a crush on him and even acted like a psycho side bitch at times. J.R. wasn't sure how she was linked to any of this, but he planned on finding out.

"She ran off huh? Y'all ain't get a chance to say nothing at all to her?" J.R. quizzed as the wheels started spinning in his head.

"Nope, the bitch was fast. We did follow her though," Lexi stated.

"Followed her where? Y'all just on y'all *Inspector Gadget* shit huh?" D'Mani laughed.

"We followed her to a house. Some man answered the door but that's all we have. We were hoping that the man was Corey, but it wasn't," Alyssa explained sadly.

"What the man looked like?" D'Mari questioned.

"It was dark, we couldn't see much but we have the address," Drea informed them.

To J.R.'s surprise, the girls actually was able to help out. He wasn't sure where their lead would lead him, but it was definitely a start. The room was quiet minus the loud snores that came from Aunt Shirley who was now knocked out sleep. It was obvious that everyone was trying to add pieces to the missing puzzle.

"We really appreciate y'all but we gotta get y'all back on with them kids," Mari stood to his feet and said as he adjusted the *Gucci* belt on his waist.

"Yeah, we gon' need the address but I promise we gon' handle shit from here," Mani too stood to his feet and spoke.

"Am I the only one with some sense? If Corey is in Mexico on business, why are they so interested in the address and who answered the door, IF they already know where he at?" Shirley popped up and said.

"But I'm just the drunk, high auntie but carry on, with y'all slow assess," she continued before loud snores captured the room once again.

***

J.R. walked through *Footlocker*, trying to decide whether he should go with the low top *Air Force Ones* or grab a pair of high-top ones. He could simply go ahead and cop both and save himself the trouble, so that's exactly what he ended up doing. After checking out at the register, he headed to the food court to grab something to drink before heading out. Checking his phone, he received a few text messages from his wife. He hit Lexi back before standing in the line at *McDonalds*. J.R. grabbed a large sweet tea with extra ice and a medium fry since he noticed they were fresh out of the grease. Heading towards the exit, he jumped on the escalator behind a group of women. J.R. couldn't help but notice how they kept looking back at him smiling. He also couldn't help but notice how thick one of the ladies was. She wasn't that cute in the face but every bitch a model when the lights were off.

"Excuse me?" he spoke, forcing them to move to the side to let him by.

***

The ladies giggled like school girls all the while eyeing him up and down. J.R. stared a little harder at the thick one. When he noticed her smiling back, he licked his lips, causing her to show every tooth in her mouth. He could easily tell that she was the leader of the pack, although she seemed shy.

"Girl, you better say something to him. He so fuck'n' fine," one of her friends cooed, causing J.R. to look at her and laugh.

"Nah, she ain't ready for me," he replied before putting some space in between them.

J.R. could hear them laughing behind him as they geeked their homegirl's head up. He knew it would only be a matter of time before she tried to prove them wrong. Just as soon as that thought entered his mind, he felt someone walking along side of him. Looking over, he spotted shorty with her phone in hand, grinning from ear to ear.

"What's up? You finna give me yo number?" he looked over and asked.

"Why? You want it?" she quizzed, trying too hard to flirt.

"Yeah, gon' give it to me," he told her, pulling his phone from his pocket.

J.R. stored her number as she ran off the digits.

"Aight baby. I'm going to hit your line...."

He paused, remembering he had yet to get her name.

"Deana, my name is Deana," she assured him.

"Aight beautiful, I'm going to hit your line later," J.R. replied with plans on keeping his word.

❧ 14 ❧

Mari walked in the room and stripped out of his clothes and headed straight for the shower. He needed to wash the day's events away and get ready for the next day. Taking lives of others wasn't something that D'Mari was proud of, but with the life that he lived, the shit was inevitable. As soon as he stepped in the shower, Drea walked in.

"You still mad at me?" she asked as she got undressed and stepped in the shower with him.

"I ain't mad... was just a little frustrated because you and your sister so fuckin' hardheaded... it ain't like we ain't know that shit, but we just assumed... hoped... that y'all would let us handle this shit and protect y'all," Mari explained.

"I know baby, but look on the bright side... we helped y'all out. Y'all probably hate to admit it, but we know that address is gonna come in handy for y'all in some kinda way."

He knew that Drea was trying to get information, but he wasn't going. The least she knew the better. By the girls getting that address, the guys were able to locate Deana and she had told them everything that they needed to know.

"Y'all did come through, but for real... y'all gotta fall back and let u work," Mari commanded.

"We will babe... and I'm sorry. I'm sorry for everything. I'm just ready to get back to normal," Drea confessed.

Mari knew that *the normal* she spoke of was probably years and years away, but he hoped that they could at least handle their current issues soon and very soon. He didn't want to die in the streets, but he knew that he also had a few years left to ensure they had a solid future for their family. Normally, his silence would prompt a hundred more questions, but it did the exact opposite at that moment. Mari was super shocked when Drea dropped to her knees and swallowed his dick. He felt it as it grew inside of her wet mouth and by instinct, his hand went to her head. Mari fucked her mouth and she welcomed the shit. Drea licked and sucked on his dick and balls and Mari fought hard to keep his balance. It wasn't until she had his balls and dick in her mouth when he lost it and slipped. It didn't stop his wife though; she sucked him until he came and swallowed every single drop of his cum.

"Got damn girl!" he grunted after he finally caught his breath.

Drea helped him up and then they washed each other off and finally got out of the shower. After drying off, Mari slipped on pair of black *Polo* boxers and laid across the bed. Him and the guys said that they would meet up to discuss how they would handle shit, but Mari decided that it could wait until the next day. He picked up his phone and made a FaceTime to call to his mom and talked to the kids for a few minutes. It dawned on him that his own mama didn't have his back either. The damn Holiday's had rubbed off on her ass. Corey was on D'Mari's mind twenty-four seven and he prayed that his cousin was alright. All of a sudden, Mari got the feeling that they needed to make a move right then instead of waiting. He grabbed his phone and sent a text to the guys in the new chat they made without Corey for obvious reasons.

Mari: I got a feeling we need to make a move NOW!!

Mani: Damn man... Stasia gon be trippin.

J.R.: Lexi is too, but I'm wit it... I can't rest until we get that nigga back and who knows if them niggaz gon keep moving the same.

Mari: Let's ride out in ten minutes. We can take two cars just in case anything goes wrong and we gotta split up.

J.R.: Bet

Mani: Aight

Mari got up and walked into the closet and got dressed in all black. It was a little after ten when he looked at his phone. Drea was still in the bathroom doing her hair since it had gotten wet in the shower. The blow dryer went off and he knew that he was about to get a whole line of questioning. Instead of waiting on her to appear, he walked towards the bathroom to get the conversation over with.

"Babe... we gotta make a run," he kissed her and waited for the twenty-one questions that he knew were coming, but instead Drea shocked him.

"Please be safe baby," she told him.

"I will... be back soon," Mari said and turned to leave.

Before he could reach the door, Drea called out to him and he knew that it was too good to be true.

"I got my lawyer friend ready for J.R. Let me know the details."

"Oh, we got it handled... I meant to tell you not to worry about it. My bad," he assured her and walked out.

Shit was too good to be true with Drea and Mari hoped that the rest of the night went that way as well. He met Mani and J.R. in the living room and they were dressed in all black as well.

"Ya'll ready?"

"Ready as we gon' get."

"Hell yeah!"

"I'm goin' too," Aunt Shirley's voice rang out from the kitchen.

"Y'all come on... we just gotta ignore her drunk ass right now," Mani said.

"Ain't nobody..."

The door slammed before they could hear the rest of what she saying and Mari laughed. He went and hopped in his truck and J.R. got in with him. When he pulled out, D'Mani was right behind him. Mari already had the address programmed into his GPS because he knew that they would be using it soon, so he hit it and followed the directions. Twenty minutes later, they were almost there and he called Mani on speaker and they discussed last minute details. Mari parked down the street while Mani went and parked on the street in front of the house. It was decided that Mani would stay outside and come in later. They needed eyes everywhere and since it was only two men in the house, according to Deana, Mari and J.R. were more than confident in handling them.

When they moved the flower pot, the key was right under it just like Deana said. Mari almost felt a little bad about having to kill the bitch, but that feeling didn't last long. She should have never aided in kidnapping his cousin and they wouldn't even be in the predicament that they were in. J.R. and Mari made their way inside and headed straight for the kitchen and looked for the basement door. Each of them had a gun in both hands as they opened the door and made their way down. They descended the steps prepared to save their boy, but willing to die in the process because you never knew how shit was going to play out.

Before Mari made it the final step, J.R. had already started shooting. Out of the corner of his eye, he spotted Corey in the corner tied up and with his head, he was motioning towards the other corner. Mari looked and saw someone running out of the door. He knew that it had to be Larry because Julian was on the floor laying in a puddle of blood.

"Fuck... that nigga got away. Let's get Corey and get the fuck outta here."

"I'm emptying both clips in this fuck boy!" J.R. spat and did just that.

Julian's face was almost unrecognizable by the time J.R. was done. Not knowing what or who else might have been in the house, the guys left right after untying Corey. When they made it outside, Mani's car was speeding away.

❧ 15 ❧

D'Mani sat outside waiting to see if the information the sisters had given them would be helpful. He really didn't want to be the one left outside but it wasn't gonna take all of them to get Corey out of there. Not if Larry and Julian was all they had to worry about. He really couldn't believe that Julian had been a part of that shit. It wasn't like they were close or nothing but the level of *disloyalty* that they were encountering just kept on shocking him.

D'Mani shifted in his seat and glanced at the door again before returning his attention back to his phone. Anastasia had been texting him damn near every other minute trying to find out what was going on. She was starting to make him wish he'd just went ahead and left his phone or cut that shit off.

Stasia: Y'all ok?
Stasia: Ik you see me textin you D'Mani
Stasia: You could at least say you're ok
Me: We fine
Stasia: You ain't gotta say it like that

Instead of continuing to go back and forth with her, he

decided to go ahead and block her number until later. He couldn't afford to cut his phone off just in case D'Mari and JR needed him and couldn't just run out. The way things were going, it was no telling what other problems they might encounter. At that point, D'Mani wasn't putting shit past anyone or any situation.

Looking at the clock, he realized that a whole ten minutes had gone by and he still hadn't seen any movement. *What the fuck them niggas in there doin'?* D'Mani thought, and no sooner than it crossed his mind, he saw someone jumping the fence out of the yard.

He leaned closer and could see Larry's overweight ass running like his life depended on it and it definitely did. D'Mani was so caught off guard by him just running out that he didn't have time to pull his gun out before that nigga was behind the wheel of a dark gray Impala squealing away. Without thinking, he took off behind him and busted a right at the corner, bumping his rear end hard enough to make him swerve slightly. That nigga drove like he worked for NASCAR though and sped right up while D'Mani straightened his wheel.

"*Fuck!*" He cursed angrily as he tried to pick back up speed. You would have thought that he was the one that was rear ended, but in his defense, it wasn't everyday he was out in the streets chasing niggas down in cars and shit. He was used to pulling up on a nigga wherever they were at and laying them down, but this shit wasn't his thing.

Larry continued speeding and whipping corners, not giving a fuck about any of the people that they passed and damn near hit--which was probably the reason that he was getting away because D'Mani was trying his hardest to avoid them. His phone rang further distracting him, but at the sight of his brother's name, he answered and put it on speaker.

"Aye we got Corey, but that fat mutha fucka got away!" D'Mari said as soon as the call connected. A feeling of relief flowed through his body hearing that their cousin was good, but it was still a matter of catching up to Larry's slick ass.

"Bet... but I'm right behind that nigga Larry now!"

"What?!" He could hear them talking in the background as his brother told everybody to get into the other car that they had come in. "Where ya at?"

D'Mani tried to find the exact name of the street that they were on, but they were going too fast and he didn't know the streets well enough yet to know exactly where he was. He quickly described his surroundings the best that he could.

"I know exactly where ya at... y'all ain't get too far bro... we on the way!" He heard JR say in the background before he left the phone fall from between his ear and shoulder. Just a second before, it seemed like Larry was going to stay straight, but at the last second, he hit a quick right. In the midst of D'Mani trying to follow suit, he lost control of the wheel.

The car did a series of spins, bumping the tail end of one car and sending a truck into the other lane before riding up onto the curb and into a fire hydrant. As a crowd of onlookers gathered around and the shrieks died down, D'Mani punched the steering wheel angrily. He already knew that half the people out there had their phones out ready to record anything that may happen after such a big accident. The beater he was driving wasn't a concern because the shit was traceless, but he still needed to get out that bitch and walk away without being seen. But he just ain't see how that was going to happen.

Cursing under his breath, he threw his hood up and sent a text to D'Mari to tell him what street he was on since he'd gotten into the accident right on the corner. Once he was confident that they would be able to grab him around the corner, D'Mani stuffed his phone in his pocket and stepped out of the car.

"Hey! Hey get back here! You hit my car buddy!"

D'Mani heard the man behind him yelling and continued to walk away briskly as people around them either mumbled or tried to call out for him to stop. He picked up his step and brushed past the crowd on the sidewalk, making sure to keep his head down and his face shielded by the hood. Thankfully they all had enough sense to let him go on about his way because he would hate to have had to pull out his gun to get out of there, but he would have.

The walk to the corner was full of him silently chastising himself over letting that nigga get away. It was like he'd had him right there and then his ass pulled some old Dukes of Hazard shit on him. D'Mani was more than angry. He was enraged almost to the point where his vision was blurry.

It wasn't until he climbed into the car with JR, his brother, and Corey that he realized it was because at some point, he'd hit his head on the steering wheel.

"Damn nigga what the fuck happened to yo head?" D'Mari asked as soon as they pulled off. Confused, D'Mani pulled out his phone and saw that he had a gash on his forehead that was leaking blood. He thought that it was sweat running down his face after speed walking with that damn hood up. He shook his head and released a deep sigh still pissed off, but glad to see his cousin still breathing beside him.

"That fuckin' accident man! I was so close to that fat fuck!" he fumed.

"Don't trip bro," D'Mari said in a low tone as they made their way home. He may have been saying that, but D'Mani knew that everybody in the car was heated. They had to get Larry's slick ass before he got them. It just seemed easier said than done.

16

Feeling the sharp pains in his back, chest, and stomach, Corey could no longer sleep comfortably. Slowly getting out of bed, he limped to the bathroom to examine the work the doctor had done the night before. Cringing at his reflection, Corey noticed two sets of stitches on both sides of his head. The gash on the right side of his head was worse than the one on his left. Both of his eyes were black but the right one was damn near closed. Lifting up his wife beater, Corey placed his hand on the bandages that were wrapped around him. The doctor that examined Corey told him that if he would've taken one more blow to his ribs, they would've been fractured.

"Shiiittt!" he yelled out in pain.

Quickly walking over to the nightstand, Corey searched for the Perks that doctor gave him for the pain, and when he saw that they were gone, he cussed some more.

"Baby, I hear you all the way down the hall. What's wrong?" Alyssa entered the room with a tray full of food and a Wal-Mart bag hanging from her wrist.

"I need them Perks. Where they at?"

"In the trash," she spoke calmly, sitting the tray on the bench at the foot of the bed.

"What! Alyssa, I need—"

"You don't need shit! I know the doctor gave them to you for your pain, but the last thing I need is for you to be addicted to that shit again. You hear me?" his wife pointed at him.

Briefly remembering the encounter he had with the pills, Corey nodded his head.

"Now, I brought you a few things to help with your pain. When you get finished eating, I'm gonna run you a hot bath. Aight?"

"Okay bae."

Alyssa fixed the pillows on the bed so Corey could sit up comfortably to eat. Placing the tray in front of him, he silently blessed the food before taking a fork full of pancakes. With Corey only eating once in the past few days, he devoured most of food his in fifteen minutes. Too focused on the food in front of him, he didn't notice the tears rolling down his wife's face until he heard her sniffle.

"Aww Lyssa," he moved the tray to the side. "Come here bae."

Alyssa slid closer to him, placing her head on his shoulder.

"I know you were worried sick about me bae, but I'm home now."

"Corey, you were *kidnapped and tortured*. Look at you. You look like Martin when he got his ass whooped by Tommy Hearns," she wiped the tears from her eyes.

Corey couldn't help but to chuckle thinking about the episode.

"If I wouldn't have sent you to the gas station, this shit wouldn't have happened."

"Wait a minute, Lyssa! I know you haven't been blaming yourself for what happened to me?"

She didn't respond.

"Aww baby. What happened to me had nothing to do with you. Aight? What I need to know is why you here without my daughter?" he glanced down at her.

"Ya brothers sent us to Mississippi with the kids, but we came back here to help find you."

Taken aback by her answer, Corey lifted her chin for her to look at him.

"Y'all came back *here* looking for me?"

"You're *my* husband Corey, and we all knew them niggas were lying when they said you went on a trip."

Kissing her on the forehead, they embraced in a brief hug before Alyssa headed to the bathroom to run the water for his bath. Corey finished up the last of his food then made his way to the bathroom. Alyssa helped him disrobe, removed his bandages, and helped him in the tub. The water was extremely hot, but it felt good on his body. After leaving him to soak in the tub for twenty minutes, Alyssa returned to wash him up, and then she dried him off and placed a few heating strips on his back before reapplying his bandages. When she was finished, Alyssa informed him that she was leaving to get him a new phone before kissing him good-bye. Throwing on another wife beater, a pair of ball shorts, socks and *Nike* slides, Corey headed down stairs to the basement where his brothers were.

Upon entering the man cave, he was greeted with weed smoke and shook his head at J.R., who was cussing Mani out.

"Nigga, I swear ya ass be cheating! Ain't no way you just beat me 42-17!"

"Aww nigga. Quit ya whining. You already knew what it was before you hopped on the controller," Mani dismissed him.

"Do that shit with me nigga. I got next," Corey cockily spoke.

"Will you be able see with ya eye damn near shut, bro?" Mani joked.

"Start the game and let's find out."

"But on some serious shit man. How you feeling?" J.R. inquired.

"Besides the pain and physical appearance, I'm cool. Just glad to be alive man," Corey took a seat on the couch next to Mari.

"I hear that. So, what the fuck they grab you for?" Mari hit the blunt before passing it to Mani.

"To get me to join their little team and snitch on y'all."

"What the fuck?" J.R. shouted.

"Yeah. The nigga Julian told Larry about us, and when he found out I was a part of the Rock Boyz, it must've been around the time he first introduced himself to me. That nigga was volunteering info because he wanted me to do something for him in return, which was for us to join forces to take down the Tessa cartel."

"I knew that grimy ass nigga wanted something yo," Mani shook his head.

"So when you told them that shit wasn't gonna happen, they fucked you up and tried to bribe you to join their team?" Mari asked.

"Pretty much. Them niggas tried to play me like I was a straight *pussy ass* nigga. Especially Julian's bitch ass. The nigga was getting mad because I wouldn't fold. He really wanted to kill my ass but Larry told him to chill."

"Did that fuck nigga say why he set me up?"

"Yeah. Because you called him in as a backup for me. He felt like he shoulda been a part of our operation from the jump. The nigga felt disrespected," Corey shrugged.

"True fuck boy shit," J.R. chuckled. "Did that nigga Larry say why he wanted to take down the Tessa's?"

"He said them niggas accused him of stealing and shit,

and when he proved to them that it wasn't him, they still kicked him out. He blamed the Tessa's for his downward spiral in life and wants revenge."

"We're gonna have to find that nigga soon. Depending on how much Julian told him, Larry could be a problem for us," Mari stated.

The brothers nodded their heads in agreement. After chopping it up for a few more minutes, Corey questioned returning to the streets after what happened to him but decided against it. Him leaving now would be like running away, and after the hell and torture they put his ass through, he'd be a damn fool to leave before Larry was killed.

❧ 17 ❧

"**I**t's sooooo boring here. When can we come back home?"

J.R. listened as Yasmine whined into the phone. According to his little sister, Mississippi was boring and too hot for her liking. He knew she was displeased with the idea from the beginning but like everyone else, she didn't have a choice either.

"You aint got much longer Yas." He said, grabbing the blunt from Lexi.

"Yeah, whatever.... Bye." She mumbled under her breath before ending the call.

Dealing with nothing but women and their fuck'd up attitudes made him miss his son even more. Outside of the guys, he knew Amir would be his best friend. He planned on teaching his son shit that he never learned as a kid. He vowed to never allow Amir to get caught up in the streets like he did. J.R. planned on molding his son young, he wondered if he had the same type of father figure in his life, if he would have turned out different.

"You good?"

Lexi's voice snapped him out of his trance. He had been so wrapped up in his thoughts, he forgot that she was right there.

"Yeah, I'm straight." He lied, turning to look at her.

"You sure, cuz you aint passed the blunt yet." She laughed.

It hadn't dawned on him that he was that much into his thoughts. He took a look at the blunt and then at Lexi.

"Wait. How long you been back smoking?" he quizzed.

"Since you been stressing me the fuck out." she admitted, snatching the blunt out his hand.

J.R. knew he had been putting a lot of unnecessary stress on the people he loved. He had no idea that the street shit would get out of hand the way it did. They had been dodging a lot of bullets and getting lucky, but he had to make sure things was handled before their luck ran out.

"Baby, I love you. I promise, everything gon be ok." Lexi stated, rubbing his back.

"I love you too baby." He smiled, turning to his new wife.

J.R. knew he was going have to show Lexi how much she really meant to him after everything was said and done. She had proved to be a true rider and for that, he owed her the world. He was going to start things off with a huge wedding and a honeymoon in Paris. After that was out of the way, he planned on giving her at least four more babies. Having a huge family was always something that he wanted.

Lexi and J.R. smoked while watching old episodes of Good Times. He low-key missed when life was that simple. He missed not having to look over his shoulder and needing security to protect his woman when he was not around. Things had changed drastically for him, now he was wondering if it was worth it.

J.R. started to doze off when his phone vibrated. He knew it was a text message, so he ignored it until it sounded again.

"If you don't, I will." Lexi said, reaching under the pillow and handing him the phone.

J.R. felt Lexi breathing down his neck as he opened it. He had nothing to hide, therefore, he let messy Lexi do her thang. After unlocking the phone, J.R. went to his messages and read it.

Mani: Meet me in the basement.

"Meet me in the basement huh? Is that some type of secret bro code for cheating?" she asked, tossing the covers off of her.

J.R. paused all movement and stared at her. The street shit had her paranoid for all the wrong reasons. The last thing on his mind was pussy, as a matter of fact, Lexi and her six weeks was coming to an end, real soon.

"I'll be back." he said, before heading out of the room.

He heard Lexi smacking her lips and carrying on, but he ignored her and kept it moving. J.R. maneuvered through the house and made it to the basement where he found the rest of the guys. As usual, someone was pouring shots while D'Mari rolled up a blunt. Drinking and getting high had become second nature to the guys. Liquor and weed seemed to be the only thing that kept them level headed and to be perfectly honest, that was a temporary.

"It took you long enough." Mani looked up from the pool table and stated, before sinking a ball in the corner pocket.

"Nigga, what I tell you about sending me those gay ass messages?" He barked, causing everyone to laugh.

"I only told yo hoe ass to meet us down here. What's gay about that?" he quizzed.

"Yo ass been suspect since you rode that horse on the beach." J.R. replied.

The entire basement, erupted in laughter as they each remembered the time they went to Jamaica with their women.

"Man fuck you. My girl wanted to do that shit." Mani said in his defense, but it only made everyone laugh harder.

J.R. sat down and joined his brothers as they talked about their next moves. Each guy agreed that the girls needed to leave before more shit hit the fan. As far as the nigga Larry, they still had no solid leads on him but J.R. knew exactly where to go for resources so they headed out.

Corey drove as the guys pulled up to a huge black gate in a gated community about forty-five minutes from Atlanta. J.R. sat in the front seat and looked around, making sure to always be aware of his surroundings. Nudging Corey with his elbow to hit the intercom button, a male with a heavy Spanish accent answered.

"Jessica Ortiz." J.R. spoke and waited for a reply but instead, the gates opened, allowing them access inside.

Circling around the neighborhood, they finally stumbled across the address. Corey pulled in front of a two- story brick home behind a white Benz and killed the engine.

"You sure this the crib?" Mani asked from the backseat.

"Yeah, this what she gave me." He replied, looking in his phone and checking the text message again.

"This bitch living good. Let's ride." Mari stated, opening his door first and stepping out.

The guys stepped over the manicured lawn, heading towards the front door when it opened before they could make it to the porch. Two huge black men appeared, one stood in the doorway, while the other stepped onto the porch, both with assault rifles in hand. J.R. turned to look at his brothers, all of them with the same puzzled look on their faces.

"Rock Boyz, Ms. Ortiz is expecting you."

The big fella at the door, moved to the side, allowing them entrance inside the beautiful home. Each guy took their turn scoping out the place. Making mental notes of how many people was around and where the closest exits were, just in case.

"Ms. Ortiz is in her study, go in." the same guy as before instructed, pointing down a long hall to a closed door.

Doing exactly as they were told, J.R. knocked on the door and seconds later, it opened.

"Well look who finally came to pay me a visit." Jessica said, opening her arms wide, welcoming J.R. in for a hug.

After falling into her embrace, J.R. introduced her to the guys before getting right down to business. Each of them, took turns filling her in on everything that was happening, from Corey being kidnapped up to all the current events. Jessica listened attentively, shaking her head up and down, not once uttering a word. Once the guys were done summing things up, she finally spoke.

"As you already know, Larry ran with the Tessa Cartel. Everything you've said is true. They kicked him out, he fell on his ass and revenge has been his only mission. Larry has a way of manipulating people. He knows how to get inside a person's head and twist all their thoughts. Not only is a con artist, he's very smart and detailed. Tessa Cartel used him as the brain of the operations because he was always a few steps ahead of everything and everyone. I'm going to let yall know now, getting to him, will not be an easy task." She explained.

"We see that now." Mari chimed in.

"Hell yeah but aint no nigga walking God's green Earth untouchable." J.R. added.

"This is true." She agreed with a head nod.

"So, what we gotta do to ensure this nigga is six feet under?" Corey quizzed.

Jessica looked at each of them briefly before addressing Corey's question.

"You gotta beat him at his own game. Simple as that. But it won't be easy. I can give yall all the info needed but if yall don't strategically approach him, you are going to fail each time."

Jessica continued, providing them with vital information on Larry. In fact, J.R. was pretty sure she was telling everything that she knew, he just hoped it worked. They guys sat around, listening to her and drinking for about another hour before they left. Each of them thanked her individually before dipping out. Jessica walked them to the door but called out for J.R. to come back. After telling the guys, he'll catch up to them, he went to see what Jessica had say.

"I know we met on the worst terms possible, but I would sacrifice my life all over again if that meant helping you. I just want you to know that the love I've always had for your mom has poured onto you and I'm going to always be here for you. I didn't want to say this in front of the guys but, you all might be in over ya head trying to get Larry. There's only one person who I know can kill Larry without breaking a sweat and that's your father. You should really reach out to him for help."

J.R. listened until she was done but the moment, she mentioned his father, it was a wrap. There was no way in hell he was hitting him up. J.R. felt like at that point, him and Tessa's Cartel beef was done. Justin spared Yasmine's life and for that, he would forever be grateful, but hell would freeze over before him and that man worked side-by-side.

❦ 18 ❦

The guys sat around the table at HS4 waiting on a little more time to pass before they made a move. Drinks were flowing and the music was blasting. The couples were enjoying a nice night out, but little did the sisters know, they had to head out soon to follow up on the lead that Jessica had given them. Mari couldn't remember the last time that they all had been at Lexi's club together, but he had to admit, they were all having a good ass time. Drea had gone with Lexi to her office, but Lyssa and Stasia were right under their men. Mari understood why, considering the circumstances. Mari looked towards the stage and saw a different stripper was putting on a show. He had to admit, she was doing her thang.

"Want me to go take her place?" Drea appeared and whispered in his ear.

"Go head... I got some cash to sling your way," he joked.

Drea turned and headed towards the stage, but Mari grabbed her arm and pulled her back.

"Sitcho ass down girl," he laughed.

He could literally see her ass tryna get on stage just to prove a point.

"You don't wanna see what Baby Holiday taught me?" Drea smirked.

"I do, but you can show me later... not the whole club," he pulled Drea on his lap and kissed her.

"I got you babe," she purred.

"Get a roooom!" Lexi squealed and Drea flipped her off.

"Here's another round for you guys," the waitress appeared and started passing out their drinks.

Mari had to admit, Lexi and J.R. did a great job with the staff they had on board. You would think that the girl was only providing great service to them because of who they were, but the truth was, the entire staff was walking around serving and making those tips.

"It's been a long ass time since I been in my muthafuckin' establishment, so let's toast to me being here," Lexi held her shot glass of.

"This yo last shot... you know you can't handle that *Patron* anyway," J.R. told her.

"Whatever... hold y'all damn glasses up."

They all did as Lexi instructed and took their shots to the head. Mari felt his phone vibrating and knew that it had to be the alarm that he set. He gave his boys the signal and they all wore the same expressions on their faces.

"Babe, come on let me holla at you for a min," he whispered in Drea's ear.

Mari led Drea near the bathroom where the music wasn't so loud. He could tell that she was feeling the effects of the alcohol by her body language. Drea hugged him and began kissing on his neck.

"Don't start nothing in this club you can't finish."

"Oh, I can finish it," Drea proclaimed.

"Aight aight... I believe you, but listen up babe," Mari

spoke as he grabbed her hands that had found their way towards his dick.

"Remember when we agreed to let y'all stay, we said we still had shit to do right?"

"Yeah, I remember."

"Well, this is one of those times. When y'all leave here, security will be following y'all... so go straight to the mansion. Please keep your sister in line babe. We don't need any distractions," Mari pleaded.

"Okay, I got you baby," Drea replied and gave him a kiss.

"Thanks love... I'll be back soon. I love you."

"I love you more," Drea replied and Mari made his way towards the exit.

Mari hopped in his truck and about ten minutes later, everyone was inside. He was glad that he thought ahead and gave everyone extra time to talk to their women. For the second time, Drea had shocked the hell out of him with being so understanding, but he was thankful as hell for it.

"I knew it was gon' take y'all asses a minute to get ya women in check... y'all gotta be more like me," Mari joked as he put the truck in gear and drove away.

"Shut the fuck up nigga."

"You swear."

Mani and J.R. replied.

"Lyssa damn shol' didn't wanna let me leave," Corey sighed.

"We figured that she would be the toughest, but Drea gon' keep 'em all in line. And Corey, you can be the lookout guy this time just because you still beat up and shit," Mari explained.

Corey agreed and Mari continued on towards one of the houses that Jessica told them Larry owned that no one knew about. The way that she described it to J.R., it was out in the country and very secluded. The guys figured they could catch him late at night, kill him in his own damn house, and leave him there.

"I really wanna be the one to kill that nigga, but as long as he dies I'm good," Corey spoke after a few minutes of silence.

"Aight check this, after we kill the nigga, we'll let you come in and empty your clip in him... it'll still make ya feel better. You saw how I did Julian bitch ass," J.R. said.

"Bet that up," Corey replied.

About twenty minutes later, they were nearing the address and the shit was exactly how Jessica said it would be.

"Jessica ain't let me down yet. I'm glad I didn't kill her ass," J.R. verbalized.

"Shiidddd... we all glad," Mari turned the lights off and parked on the side of the road.

The walk wouldn't be too far, but Corey would be on standby if anything went wrong. Mari, Mani, and J.R. made their way towards the house and there was only one car parked on the side. The three of them split up once they reached the house to check shit out. It wasn't anything fancy, just like Jessica said, but it was one of the places Larry felt safe.

"That nigga ain't in there or he knocked the fuck out. Ion see no movement," J.R. expressed when they met back in the front.

"Well it's show time. Gon' and see if that key code works or if we gotta make some noise on the way in," Mani chimed in.

They looked on as J.R. entered the code that Jessica had given him and *wala*, they were in. There was no movement in the living room, but a radio could be heard coming from towards the back. J.R. kicked the door open and started shooting instantly. Mari and Mani followed suit, but when feathers started flying around, they knew it wasn't Larry that they were shooting. J.R. made his way towards the made-up body and picked up a piece of paper.

"Yooo get the fuck out y'all!!" J.R. yelled and all the guys took off running. As soon as they made it outside and ran about a hundred feet, the house blew the fuck up.

"FUCCKKK!! This nigga smarter than we thought," J.R. fussed when they made it back to the truck.

They watched as the house continued burning and finally drove away feeling defeated as fuck.

❧ 19 ❦

D'Mani was still upset about letting Larry get away, getting in that accident, almost blowing up in that damn house, but shit still had to keep moving. Corey had let them in on as much as he could about what Larry, Julian, and Deana had going on but it wasn't much. They were basically still trying to follow leads. With everything that had been going on, he still had yet to deal with Cheyanne's remains, and as much as he didn't want to have to deal with that shit, he needed to get it done. *That* day.

After getting dressed in some black *Nike* joggers and a white tee, he changed the bandage on his forehead and got ready to leave the house, but Stasia walked into the room.

"Where you headed?" she asked, laying on top of the bed and stretching.

"I gotta go take care of Cheyanne's remains and--"

"You got time for a quickie?" The look on her face let him know that that was the whole reason that she'd come in there in the first place. He was honestly surprised that it had taken her so long say something. Sex was big for them and the way shit had been going made them being in the mood infrequent at best. Despite his mood, he couldn't help but grin as she crawled across the bed to him without waiting on a response and reached inside of his sweats.

"Damn, you ain't even gone let me answer before you just come take it huh?" She had already released him from both the joggers and his boxers with a smirk of her own. Dipping her head, she ran her tongue along his shaft from his nuts to the tip, stopping to suck the head softly.

"You want me to stop?" she teased weakly, pretending to pull away but he quickly put a stop to that.

"Hell naw... you gotta finish now."

She giggled, knowing that she had broken him down in a matter of seconds, but he planned on getting her back before they were done. With his dick now at full length, he squeezed his eyes shut and tried to control himself while she went to work, slurping and jacking him off. It had been so long that he was already on the verge of coming and she hadn't really even done shit.

In order to take control of the situation and his nut, Mani pulled away and helped her to lay back on the bed before snatching his shirt over his head. The crotch of her nude biker shorts was drenched and he was already consumed with feeling that wetness sliding up and down the length of his dick. She removed her own shirt while he helped her out of them tight ass pants she wore.

The closer he brought his face to her center, the more Stasia began to pant, anticipating the feel of his tongue. He started to play like he wasn't about to continue, but her reaction to his head always boosted his ego and he'd rather see that. After he took the rest of his clothes off, he bent and dipped his tongue inside of her nectar, causing her to coo in response.

"Oooh shit!" she hissed, egging him on. He stuck a finger and then another inside of her and continued to suck on her clit, alternating between being gentle and being rough. She came fast and hard and was still recovering when he sat up and slid inside of her.

"God damn!" D'Mani hadn't realized that he'd missed fucking her so much until she'd come in there teasing him. Now it was almost like he couldn't get enough. He lifted one of her legs over his shoulder so that he felt all of her, and he damn near drowned from how wet she was. The room was filled with the sound of him sliding through her soft walls, further pushing him to his limit. B he knew it, they were both releasing at the same time.

D'Mani fell over next to Stasia as they both breathed heavily, trying to return their breathing back to normal. After a second, their eyes met and they both burst into laughter.

"You was *pressed* for that dick wasn't you?" he joked, cheesing and putting his arms behind his head before Anastasia mushed him in the head with a playful expression of her own.

"Don't do me, you wanted it too."

"Maybe a little. Ow... ayite!" She had pinched his side with them sharp ass claws.

"Ayite what?" she pressed.

"I *needed* that shit too," he admitted, giving her a stern look. As hard as she had pinched him, he was sure that their grandkids would feel that shit.

"See that's all you had to say," she quipped, unfazed by his glare and then snuggled closer.

Before D'Mani knew it, they had both fallen asleep when just a second before he was on his way out the door. By the time they woke up, he only had an hour left before the funeral home would be closing. He left Stasia in bed snoring and hurried out the door, not seeing anybody around the house.

D'Mani made it to the funeral home with ten minutes

before they would close and rushed inside. The front area of the place was eerily silent and a chill ran over his body the further inside he came. Instead of looking for someone to help, he started hitting the bell that sat on the desk. Thankfully an old ass black dude was still there. He shuffled behind the desk and D'Mani was glad that he got right to business, which meant he'd be leaving that much sooner.

After he made plans to have her cremated, he went to go talk to a tech guy he knew of. He hoped that maybe they could track Corey's old phone since Larry used it to send him texts. He made it to Wayne's house pretty quickly and stepped onto his broken up porch.

"Wassup man?" Wayne said, answering the door.

"Shit you tell me," D'Mani looked down at the tight ass pants he wore and frowned while Wayne laughed unbothered.

"Man let me live." D'Mani didn't say nothin' else, but he wasn't blind to how *feminine* Wayne acted. It wasn't his problem though. As long as he did what he was paid for, his business was his own.

"Live ya life," D'Mani said, throwing his hands up as he followed him inside. Once they made it to Wayne's high tech room that was full of big screen computers and spyware shit, he took a seat in what looked like a gaming chair.

"So what brings you by?"

"I'm tryna track this number and see if we can find out its location," D'Mani explained, handing over his phone with the number displayed. Wayne inspected it for a second before turning around and typing it into the computer he sat at. D'Mani watched closely, unsure of what all of the shit on the screen meant.

"You wanted an address right?" Wayne asked, looking over his shoulder. At the mention of an address, D'Mani leaned closer to the screens.

"Hell yeah!" This seemed like the closest they'd gotten

since rescuing Corey, but his excitement immediately died down when Wayne pointed out the address on the screen. It was the same place they'd gotten Corey from and he knew it wasn't no way Larry went back there. Disappointed, D'Mani paid the man and mentally scratched the phone off his list of possible leads. It was starting to seem like that nigga was *untouchable*, even though he had the phone location tracked on a whim. As bad as shit seemed, he was just going to have to go back to the drawing board.

❧ 20 ❧

S taring up at the ceiling, Corey's frustrations with not being able to find Larry was causing him to lose sleep. Thinking back to when they were in rehab, Corey tried to remember if Larry mentioned anything about the streets that could help them find his ass but nothing rang a bell. The way Larry seemed to know what moves they were making in their search to find him pissed Corey off more and more and every time they came up short only add fuel to the fire. Thoughts of how they tortured him constantly played in his mind and he was anxious to bring Larry's life to an end. No matter how long it took.

Alyssa's movements brought Corey back to reality for a moment. He looked down at her and smiled at how she was laying on top of him with her head resting on his shoulder. Since he'd been home, his wife never wanted him out of her sight and every time he made a move, she was right there to catch him the act. Corey couldn't even go to the bathroom with Alyssa asking him where he was going. Most niggas would have told their wives to ease up but considering what he'd been through, Corey had no choice but to deal with it and checked in with her as often as he could to let her know he was cool. He had put Alyssa through a lot since they moved to Atlanta and he constantly thanked God that he still had his life *and* his wife.

Snatching his phone off the nightstand, Corey checked the time and it was 9:45am. Gently lifting Alyssa off him off, he placed her on her side of the bed before heading to the bathroom.

"Where you about to go Corey?" she mumbled before he could close the bathroom door.

"I gotta handle some business right quick."

"How long you gonna be gone?"

"I don't know. It all depends on how business is going bae, but I'll keep you posted throughout the day like I always do. Aight?"

"Okay baby," Alyssa sighed.

"What Lyssa?"

"Nothing," she huffed.

"Come on with the childish shit, Alyssa. Speak ya mind," he became annoyed.

"It's like you don't take ya life seriously, Corey. Have you not learned anything from what's happened to you?" She sat up in bed.

"I do take my life seriously. That's why I'm trying to find the nigga that's responsible for almost ending it," he raised his voice a little. "Look bae, I know you worry about me more than you ever did before, but just because I was kidnapped doesn't mean I gotta put my life on hold. I'm still gonna do whatever is needed to take care of my family. You understand me?"

"Yeah, I understand," she pouted. "I just wish it was a safer way for you to take care of ya family."

Staring at each other for a moment, Corey closed the bathroom door and pressed his head against it. No matter how strong he tried to be and stand by his reasons for staying in the game, his wife's words seemed to weaken every time she expressed her concerns to him. Corey tried to get Alyssa to see shit from his point of view but she wasn't trying to. She understood that Corey wanted revenge but all she wanted was her husband to return home to her at the end of the day.

After taking care of his hygiene, Alyssa helped him with his bandages before he got dressed for the day in a white *Polo* t shirt, black *Balmain* jeans, and wheat colored *Timberland* boots. Grabbing his *Nike* hoodie, Corey was headed out the door but his wife stopped him so they could pray together before he went out into the streets. When she was finished, he gave his wife a passionate kiss then left the house. Jumping inside his truck, Corey pulled out of the driveway and headed down the way to check on the trap houses.

Making his way to every trap house, he made sure the product was being made right and the money was on point. When Corey saw that everything was accounted for, he informed all the workers in each trap to stay on their toes at all times. With Larry still on the prowl, he didn't know what tricks that nigga had up his sleeve and he didn't want them to be caught off guard. After leaving the last trap, Corey shot a text to Alyssa letting her know that he was cool. When he received her response, another text came through from Mari asking him to check on the warehouse. He replied *okay* and drove off.

Pulling up to the warehouse a half hour later, a strange feeling caused him to drive around the entire building before parking his truck in the back of the building and removing his gun from the glove compartment. Everything was cool on the outside but when Corey entered the warehouse with his gun in hand, his mouth hit the floor at the sight before him. The blood that surrounded the dead bodies of their workers had him in a trance. The driver of the truck that was parked

inside was murdered and the truck that contain their shipment was empty. The faint coughing he heard on the other
end of the warehouse snapped Corey out of his trance.
Cautiously making his way to where the coughing came from,
he saw that it was one of the workers and placed the gun in
his waist band.

"Yo Jay? Are you hit nigga?"

"Yeah. I got hit twice. In my shoulder and my leg, but I'll
be aight though," he struggled to get up. "I thought them
niggas were gonna kill me too."

"What niggas? Who did this shit man."

"Man these niggas rolled up in this bitch like fifteen deep
and aired this motherfucka before they stole everything out
the truck. When they saw I was alive, they told me to tell
y'all that y'all had been hit by the Tessa cartel. I think that's
the only reason why they kept my ass alive. Just to make sure
you and ya brothers got that message."

"I can't believe this shit!" Corey yelled.

After making sure Jay was cool, he dashed to his car to get
his phone and called Mari.

"Wassup Cuz?"

"Nigga get to the warehouse! We just got hit!"

"I'm on my way."

Ending the call with Mari, Corey called the cleanup crew
and the doctor for the injured worker. When he walked back
into the warehouse to wait for his brothers, the cleanup crew,
and the doctor, nothing but negativity filled his head. It
seemed like shit kept going from bad to worse and besides
him being kidnapped, this shit was the worst of it all. Since
they started building their empire, this had been the biggest
L they had taken and this was something that wouldn't be
taken lightly.

"**D**O YALL HAVE ANY IDEA HOW MUCH FUCKIN' MONEY WE JUST LOST?" J.R. screamed, followed by his fist pounding into his hand.

"We all understand but hollering and shit ain't gon' solve nun."

J.R.'s head darted in the direction of the voice, his eyes landed on Big Hank, one of the security guards who was supposed to be on duty at the warehouse the day it got hit.

"What the fuck you say to me?" J.R. asked as he slowly made his way towards Big Hank.

"Look Boss, I ain't mean no disrespect but...."

Before he could finish his sentence, there was a hole in the middle of his forehead. J.R. fired one single bullet, sending him to his maker. The room remained quiet, as if everyone already seen that coming. Stepping over his body, J.R. went back to the center of the room where Corey, Mani, and Mari were still standing and joined them.

"Now, do anybody else have some shit to say?" he asked calmly, waiting for a response.

The warehouse was so quiet, you could hear a mouse piss on cotton. Everyone looked around at each other, waiting to see what was next.

"I need all eyes to the streets. If anyone sees, hears, or THINK a nigga is part of Tessa's Cartel, I need y'all to handle that... on the spot," Mari spoke.

After the meeting was adjourned, J.R. headed straight outside to his car. He almost made it safe when he heard Mari call out his name. J.R. slowed down a little, allowing him time to catch up.

"Man, you good?" Mari asked once they were side by side.

"I'm straight. You good?" he replied, looking him up and down.

"I ain't the one who just laid out an innocent moth-erfucker."

"Innocent? Yeah aight. Wad up tho?" J.R. replied, brushing him off.

"Look, I know yo head fuck'd up right now. We all dealing with some shit bro, but you need to remain level headed," Mari explained.

J.R. knew murking Big Hank was uncalled for, but he felt disrespected and now was not the time for anyone to disre-spect him.

"Look, I'll pay for the funeral and toss the family a couple of dollars but the nigga dead. Fuck you want me to do?" he snapped.

"I want you to calm the fuck down! I want you to chill. Knocking niggas heads off, that's on *your* team, is not helping. I know you frustrated cuz we thought we had this Tessa shit figured out, but now we have to act accordingly."

J.R. couldn't front. Mari made sense. He was right about the Cartel situation because in his head, he thought shit was smooth. With Justin returning Yasmine, it was like a silent truce, or so he thought. But with him stealing his work, it started a new war... a war he refused to lose.

"Mani and Corey about to check on the next shipment. Where you headed?" Mari quizzed.

"Up the block to trap house D, wanna ride with me?" J.R. asked.

Without replying, Mari hopped in the passenger's side of J.R.'s truck. The two of them sped off in the direction of the trap house. They stopped at the gas station and grabbed two bottles of water before pulling into the projects. As usual, the sidewalk was filled with kids playing, niggas shooting dice, and bitches gossiping. Both J.R. and Mari made sure their pistols was secure before exiting the ride. Feeling like neighborhood superstars, they spoke to everyone and kept it moving until a shorty who lived in the building stopped them.

"What up J.R.? What's going on Mari?" Mario spoke.

"What's up kid?" J.R. replied, giving him dap.

"Shit I can't call it. Trying to get like y'all," he praised as he admired both J.R and Mari's jewelry.

"Nah, this street shit ain't where it's at. Go to college or some shit," Mari advised.

"College? That shit ain't gon' pay my momma bills. I'm trying to get put on," he replied.

Mario had so much potential. He was the star basketball player in the district, but his fucked up upbringing led him down the wrong path.

"I heard how y'all shot up them blocks over East. Let me down, I keep the burner."

Mario lifted up the dingy white shirt he was wearing and displayed a gun at his waist.

"The way I see it, y'all gon' need some more firepower after what y'all did to Tessa's Cartel," he continued.

Before the mention of Tessa's cartel, J.R. was half ass listening but now Mario had sparked his interest.

"The fuck you talking about?" J.R. quizzed, trying to read his body language.

"Last night, Tessa's Cartel took a huge loss. Word on the street is that the Rock Boyz shot up their blocks and stole about thirty guns from them. I know the streets finna be hot now. Y'all started a war."

Both J.R. and Mari looked at each other confused. Neither of them knew what Mario was talking about but was definitely going to find out.

"Aye good-looking homie," J.R. said before going into his pocket and pilling off a couple hundred-dollar bills.

Mario thanked him and went on his way.

"Aye, where you going, thought we came to check on the trap?" Mari yelled out as J.R. turned around and headed to the car.

"That shit can wait. Text Corey and Mani and tell them to meet us at the crib ASAP!"

The duo hopped back in the truck and headed towards the mansion. With Atlanta traffic being a bitch, it took them almost an hour to get home. They used that time to try and figure out what was going on. No one gave orders to make any moves or hits on Tessa's Cartel.

Finally pulling up to the house, they parked in the back and walked around to the front. As soon as they made it to the front porch, they spotted a man sitting on the steps. Assuming it was either Corey or Mani, they proceed but got the shock of their lives when they got closer. Both men pulled their pistols out at the same time.

"Put the gun down son... I come in peace."

❧ 2 2 ❧

Both Mari and J.R. kept their guns drawn, but no fear was shown by the man that stood before them. It seemed as if a whole hour had passed, when in reality it hadn't even been thirty seconds.

"I'm gonna say it one more time, put the gun down son... and you're D'Mari or D'Mani. My first guess would be D'Mari," he spoke.

When he said *son* again, Mari finally noticed the striking resemblance of J.R. and the older man who was none other than Justin Tessa. He feared no one, but he also didn't want a blood bath right in front of the house that they had been calling home for the past few months. With those thoughts on his mind, Mari slowly lowered his gun, but J.R. continued to hold steady.

"Put it down J.R., if this man sitting on our front porch, clearly he could have been killed us if he wanted to," Mari advised his boy.

"Yeah, you're definitely D'Mari... the level headed one," Justin lightly chuckled.

His words must have resonated because J.R. followed suit and finally lowered his gun.

"What you doin' here?" J.R. quizzed.

"I think you knew that this meeting was going to come sooner rather than later. I actually expected you to reach out to me after sending Yasmine back, but instead, other shit has been going on," Justin spoke.

At the mention of Yasmine's name, Mari could see J.R. relax instantly. He knew how his homie felt about Yasmine and her returning in the midst of all of the turmoil was one of the best things that happened to J.R. and the crew. They all thought Yasmine was dead but were elated that Justin let her survive.

"I'll never be able to repay you for that... I been..."

"You don't have to. I know this isn't an ideal meeting and you don't know shit about me, but I've had my eye on you for years. Your friend is right, if I wanted you guys dead, you would've been dead. Your crew has killed both of my brothers, but I must draw the line with the large loss on money I've taken recently. I know that it wasn't The Rock Boyz, even though that's what the streets are saying. I heard about the hit you guys took as well. Larry is trying to play us against each other. The guy that you all are after is very smart, but he's not as smart as he thinks. I'm here because we need each other to kill that thieving son of a bitch once and for all. Letting him live when I cut him off is one of the biggest regrets I have in life," Justin cut J.R. off and spoke.

Mari stood there thinking about how quickly shit had changed. A few months back, they were set out to take over the streets of Atlanta and destroy the Tessa Cartel, but yet there they were, currently in negotiation with the *head* of Cartel discussing some teaming up type shit. You couldn't have paid him to think that things would have gone like they did. Mari could tell that J.R. was in deep thought just like he was by the look on his face, but he couldn't lie, it seemed like a good ass plan. Mari could see his brother having an issue with it, but the truth was, everyone wanted Larry's ass dead and no one had been successful *alone*. Neither side was weak, but they could be hell together.

"We gotta talk to the rest of the crew before we make a decision, but I'm wit it," J.R. finally replied.

"I agree. I'm wit it, but we all make decisions together."

"Well... how about y'all invite me inside, so I can look those two in their eyes while I'm here," Justin suggested.

J.R. looked at Mari and they both agreed without speaking a word. Mari fell back and allowed J.R. to lead the way inside. As soon as they walked in, Aunt Shirley was walking out of the kitchen and Mari sighed when he saw the look on her face when she saw Justin.

"Ooooh... shawty swing my way," she sang and walked up on Justin who stood there with an expression on his face that couldn't be read.

"Auntie, where's Corey and Mani?" Mari quizzed in an attempt to cut her foolishness short.

"The crackhead and the cheater down in that basement... want me to walk you down?" she grabbed Justin's hand.

"You know I like it when they play hard to get," she continued.

Justin finally gave her a weak smile.

"I like your style, but I'm gonna have to decline," he spoke and kissed her hand.

"My boyfriend down in Augusta, so if you change your mind... I'm free," Shirley winked and walked away.

Mari figured the sisters were somewhere talking and he was glad. They made their way to the basement and found Mani and Corey shooting pool. As soon as they looked up, Mani's hands went to his gun but J.R. stopped him.

"It's cool man!" J.R. announced.

"The fuck goin' on?" Mani spat.

"Justin here, who also happens to be *my Pops* and the one who saved my sister's life, wants to join forces and take Larry down. We came to see if y'all would be on board wit it," J.R. gave a brief analysis.

"We gon' get that nigga on our own. We don't need no help." Mani replied.

"Bruh, you right... we capable of doin' the shit ourselves, but at this point, we all ready to end this shit and move on with our lives. We keep coming up on dead ends. If we work together, we really can kill that nigga and get back to us," Mari expressed.

"I know everything I need to know about each of you... because of my son, I turned a blind eye to a lot of shit. I respect the business you guys are running, but let's not forget, I started the shit. The way I see it, we need each other... so, what's it gonna be?" Justin finally spoke.

Mari walked over to his twin and whispered a few words to him and he finally hopped on board.

"Aight, the way I see it... we need to inform our team on what's goin' on... you inform yours and we can all meet up?" Mani addressed Justin.

The five men agreed to meet up the following day and sealed the deal to unite with a shot of brown liquor.

23

T hings had been real funny around their camp and it was the general consensus that Larry was behind it all. First, they took that loss at the trap, and then they were being framed for robbing Justin's trap. All that time, D'Mani had thought that the nigga was extremely slick and that he'd gotten lucky; but if his plan was for both teams to take each other out, then he was much smarter than any of them thought. Even with less man power, he seemed to be two steps ahead of them every time they turned around.

The best thing at that point would be to join forces with Justin since he was coming at the both of them. That would give them bigger numbers, which meant more niggas looking for him. D'Mani wasn't exactly happy to be having to work with Justin's crew when they initially had problems; however, D'Mani and J.R. made it clear that it was for the best. In his mind, regardless an enemy would always be an enemy, but for the time being, they would have to set their differences aside. Now whether or not they were going to continue their beef once they got Larry out of the way was yet to be determined, but he was with whatever his brothers were with.

"Nigga you ready?" Corey asked him, breaking his train of thought. D'Mani hadn't realized that they had stopped at the warehouse where they were having this meeting at already. All eyes were on him as they awaited his response more than likely because he hadn't been paying attention.

"I stay ready," he finally said, pulling his gun from his hip and cocking it.

"Naw we cool, we don't need guns," J.R. commented from the front seat and D'Mari nodded in agreement. They both seemed to be on the same page about the Justin nigga. Everybody put their guns away while they waited for the few loyal members of their team that they had left since they'd arrived a few minutes early. Once they spotted the three black suburban's pull in to the huge lot, they all got out and met by the door before going inside.

Entering the warehouse, they saw Justin standing at the front of the room with his remaining men to his right. D'Mari, JR, D'Mani, and Corey lead their team to stand across from them on the other side of the room. Their faces showed their curiosity about the other team, despite the conversation that D'Mani knew that Justin had had with them before that day.

"Okay so this meeting is merely a formality. We both have an enemy at our heads and the best way we can deal with that is together." Justin started. "As of right now, neither team has been able to get their hands on this Larry nigga and we've both taken losses at his hand. Now I already talked to my team about what we're doin' here and I know y'all have had this conversation with your guys too. We got a few ways for us to work together to try and get Larry and the lil ass team he done put together."

He went on to talk about a few methods of attack that they'd be implementing; things that they had all discussed previously amongst themselves. D'Mani had been uneasy about them getting together but after talking to his brother and JR about the pros, he came around. Plus Justin had returned J.R.'s sister unharmed, so he figured he couldn't be that bad.

Not even twenty minutes later, the meeting was over and D'Mani was headed home to start sorting through Cheyanne's belongings. Things had been so hectic that he hadn't had a chance to take care of much when it came to her. It wasn't much and was mostly paperwork she had that she felt was important.

He went and checked on Stasia as soon as he got there and found her in bed asleep with drool hanging out of her open mouth. Despite all the shit that had been happening, it was good to see her sleeping so comfortable. His biggest hope was that they could get a handle on Larry so they could all sleep good. He closed the door behind him and went into the room that Cheyanne had once occupied. Even with the light on, somehow it looked dark and depressing to him. Shaking off the feeling, he began to gather her things out of the dresser drawers but stopped when he came upon a manila envelope with his name scrawled on it. Unsure of what he would find inside, he took a seat on the bed and slowly opened it up revealing a letter written in Cheyanne's neat handwriting.

Dear D'Mani,

If you're reading this, then I'm finally at rest, but I can't be at peace until I get this off of my chest. D'Mani ever since me and Imani walked into your life, you have been a Godsend and I want you to know that I truly appreciate everything that you have done for me, but I haven't been completely honest with you.

The day that we ran into each other at Wal-Mart, I was a little caught off guard and immediately told you that Imani was yours when the truth is, I'm not sure if that's true. The real reason that I left was because I was cheating on you. At the time, I thought that I deserved a 9 to 5 type of man that I wouldn't have to live in fear with and I thought I had. When I got pregnant with Imani, I wasn't sure who the father was, but I left with him hoping she was his. The fact that you and Chris favored each other made it easier for her to pass as his, and I never had any reason to get a DNA test done. He was killed in a robbery not too long after she turned one, which is why she so easily accepted you as her father. I am still unsure of whether or not she is truly yours, but he didn't have any family, and I don't want my mama or sisters to be able to use her for any money they may receive. I'm sorry for all of this, and I hope that you can find it in your heart to forgive me and not hold this against Imani. She deserves much better, and I'm hoping that you can give her that by continuing to raise her whether she is yours or not. Please look after her for me.

Sincerely Cheyanne

By the time D'Mani had finished the letter, he was more than pissed. Cheyanne had come in and wreaked havoc on his life and she didn't even know if Imani was *his*. She had put him in a fucked up position because regardless of her paternity, he had grown attached to Imani; but there was no way he could go on without knowing the truth. He abandoned what he'd been doing and went to throw the letter away. Cheyanne had really fucked him up with that shit and to know that Anastasia had been warranted in her fears and he hadn't listened was really pissing him off. He would have to keep her from ever finding out but in the meantime, he would get a paternity test and find out for himself. It was just fucked up that he was dealing with something like that in the midst of everything else, but it seemed like their lives would forever be plagued with drama.

24

Corey stared at the pictures of his baby girl that Alyssa sent to his phone and smiled. His baby girl had been in Mississippi for a couple of weeks now and he was missing his daughter something terrible. Thinking of the reason why the kids had to go away in the first place turned his smile into a tight frown. Larry was still at large and they hadn't been able to locate him since teaming up with Tessa but the workers were searching for them niggas high and low daily. Corey couldn't wait for this shit to be over so he could spend time with his baby girl again instead of looking at pictures.

Placing his phone face down in his lap, he eyed the activity the trap was getting from the middle of the block as he sat in his truck. Corey stayed posted on the block for another half hour before driving to the next trap house. The Rock Boyz had been taking shifts patrolling the traps and the warehouse to lower the risk of getting hit again. When he got to the next trap, there was more traffic on this block than the last. Parking at the end of the block, Corey killed the engine and observed. He shook his head as the fiends that couldn't afford their product offer sexual favors instead. One of his workers was about to take the woman up on her offer but quickly came to her senses and sent her ass on her way. While Corey chuckled to himself, his phone chimed indicating that he had a text message from his wife.

Lyssa: How much longer are you gonna be out?
Corey: Idk bae. Why wassup?
Lyssa: I'm horny!!

The message instantly made Corey's dick hard and before he could respond to it, Alyssa sent him a full body pick of her naked body along with a pussy pic. Licking his lips at the photos, Corey was ready to stop everything and give his wife what she wanted and then some but being as though he wasn't finished handling business yet, he had to decline her.

Corey: I love the pics Sexy but I can't get away right now but I got you as soon as I get him. Aight?
Lyssa: Okay Daddy. I'll be waiting

Staring at the pictures once more, Corey placed his phone back on his lap and continued to people watch. After an hour had passed, he started his engine and pulled off down the block. Bending the corner, Corey slammed on his brake when a young nigga darted out in front of his truck. Realizing it was a loyal customer of theirs, he rolled down his windows.

"Nigga what the fuck is wrong with you dashing out in front of the street like that?!"

"My bad O.G but I when I saw ya truck, I had to get ya attention. Pull over. I need to holla at you," the young nigga Geez told him.

Hesitant, Corey pulled over to the car and pop the locks so he could get in. Closing the door behind him, Geez reached in his pocket and revealed what was in his hand. When Corey saw that it was small clear bag with the symbol of an *ace of spade* on it, he shrugged.

"You told me to pull over so you can show me our product Geez?"

"Man, I know this y'all shit, but ya niggas ain't the ones that sold me that shit."

"What the fuck you mean?"

"I was over on the Eastside of Atlanta when a nigga told me he had that fire for sell. I told that nigga I was good, but when he offered to let me sample the shit for free, I took it and kept it moving. I examined the shit a lil while ago and when I saw the symbol, I knew this shit belonged to y'all."

Corey bit the inside of his lip as he listened to Geez. He couldn't believe that motherfucker had the audacity to try to sell their shit like it was his own.

"Do you remember what block dude was standing on?"

"Lea Drive Southwest. I'm not sure but I think it might be a trap somewhere around there," Geez answered.

"Good lookin' out Geez."

"No problem Boss."

Giving him a handshake, he took the package from Geez before he fell out of the truck. Corey locked the doors to his truck then pulled off down the block heading towards the expressway. Instead of letting his folks know what was going on, Corey decided to take the drive to find out if the information he received was legit. He made it over to the East Atlanta in twenty minutes and drove to the block that Geez gave him and sure enough, there were some niggas posted up on the corner selling work. Driving around the neighborhood, he noticed that niggas were posted up on different corners for the next two blocks. Corey waited to see if any of the block boys would dip off to their hide out but none of them move. Tired of waiting, he hopped on the expressway and headed to the mansion.

The sunset turned into night by the time he reached the mansion and Corey figured that his brothers were home.

Upon entering the crib, he made his way straight to the man cave where J.R, Mani, and Mari were smoking and drinking with T.I.'s *Motivation* playing. Taking a seat in the reclining chair, Corey took a deep breath before speaking.

"Wassup C?" Mari asked.

"Larry and his squad set up shop with *our* product in East Atlanta."

J.R. killed the music and all eyes were on him.

"What the fuck you just say?"

"Geez flagged me down when I was leaving one of the traps and told me some niggas in East Atlanta sold him our shit," he pulled the package out of his jacket pocket, placing it on the table.

They all looked at the package with their symbol on it and shook their heads.

"This nigga Larry must think we some straight pussies huh?" Mani inhaled the weed smoke.

"He must," Corey replied. "I took a ride over there to see if Geez was bullshitting and his story checked out. They definitely set up shop somewhere on the blocks they're posted up on. I just don't know which one."

"I'm tired of this bitch ass nigga being ahead of us man. We need to use this shit to our advantage and play this shit smart from here on out," Mari gulped the rest of his drink.

Everyone nodded in agreement. They chopped it up for a few minutes before Corey made his way upstairs to his bedroom where he found his wife waiting for him naked on top the blankets. Forgetting about issues with Larry, Corey kicked off his shoes, got undressed, and joined Alyssa in the bed where they fucked each other senseless for the next couple of hours.

❧ 25 ❧

J.R. zipped up his *Nike* hoodie and immediately regretted not bringing a heavier jacket. Silly of him to assume that just because it was *spring* that it would feel as such, especially in the Windy City. As soon as the doors to O'Hare airport opened, the blistering Chicago wind smacked both him and Corey in the face. The sun was shining beautifully over the city but apparently it wasn't helping with the cold temperatures.

"I don't see how people live like this all year around," Corey stated as he too zipped his hoodie up to his neck.

"Bruh, you from New York," J.R. glanced over at him and smirked as they headed to pick up the rental car.

"Yeah but this wind hit different, I ain't used to

this shit," Corey replied before joining J.R. in the *Enterprise* line.

THE TWO WAITED UNTIL THEY WERE CALLED. AFTER showing ID's and signing the necessary paperwork, they were on their way to the garage to pick up their car. Usually when they traveled, they rented something luxurious but they were there strictly on business therefore, the Nissan Maxima assigned to them was just fine. Typing the address in the GPS, J.R. headed to the West side of Chicago to pick up a few things from his homeboy Goo.

Working with little time, J.R. and Corey grabbed what they needed and headed to their next destination. They only planned on being in Chicago for a few hours; they had a return flight back to Atlanta in six hours, so they had to move quickly. Stopping off at a *McDonalds*, the both of them went inside, used the public restroom to change their clothes, and skated out.

"WE LOOKING GOOD ON TIME. HOW LONG DOES IT SAY THE drive is from here?" Corey asked from the passenger's seat.

J.R. PICKED UP HIS PHONE AND LOOKED AT THE MAP.

"ACCORDING TO THIS, WE SHOULD BE THERE IN LESS THAN thirty minutes," he confirmed.

"AIGHT BET," WAS COREY'S ONLY RESPONSE BEFORE turning up the radio and rapping along to Future.

PULLING UP TO AN ABANDONED WAREHOUSE TWENTY minutes later, J.R. unbuckled his seatbelt but kept the car running while he got out. Corey jumped in the driver's seat while J.R. used the key Goo had given him to access the People Gas truck. Once he was all settled in, he blew the horn, signaling for Corey to pull off, which he did.

J.R. followed Corey to a residential area on the Southside of the city. Double checking the address, he spotted the house and jumped out. J.R. then went around to the back of the utility truck and grabbed some cables, along with a duffle bag. Looking ahead of him, he peeped Corey walking towards him wearing the oversized navy-blue jumper that was part of his disguise. Doing the same as J.R., he too grabbed a duffle bag and cable cords before slamming the back door of the truck shut.

"YOU READY?" COREY LOOKED OVER AND ASKED.

"AS READY AS I'M GOING TO GET." HE ASSURED HIS COUSIN before walking across the dry grass to the single-family home.

"REMEMBER, IN AND OUT." J.R. REMINDED COREY WHO rang the doorbell.

COREY SHOOK HIS HEAD UP AND DOWN JUST AS THE FRONT door swung open.

TWYLA T.

"Hello ma'am, I'm Darrius with Peoples Gas," J.R. stated, pointing to the worn-out name tag on his jumpsuit.

"There's been a leakage reported in the area. We are here to make sure that everything is good on your end," Corey followed with a charming smile.

"Leakage? My God. Come in, y'all got me missing my stories," the older woman with a head full of gray hair replied before closing her housecoat shut and allowing them in.

Once inside, J.R. looked around, trying to see if she was home alone or not.

"The back door over there, gon' head and do what you gotta do," she fussed, taking a seat on the couch.

J.R. motioned with his head for Corey to look around while he went off into the kitchen. Once Corey reported back to him that they were in fact alone, J.R. went to work. Grabbing the cordless house phone off the wall, he headed back towards the living room with it in hand.

"I hope y'all done," the elderly lady hissed from the couch, looking up briefly at J.R.

SHE MUST HAVE NOTICED EITHER THE LOOK ON HIS FACE OR phone in his hand, either way, it sparked her interest.

"WHAT THE FUC— WHY YOU....." SHE STUTTERED AS SHE struggled to stand to her feet.

"SHUT THE FUCK UP BITCH!" J.R. BARKED, PUSHING her back on the couch and tossing the phone in her lap.

"CALL YO BITCH ASS SON," COREY SPOKE, WALKING CLOSER to the older woman.

"MY—MY—MY SON. WHAT DOES HE HAVE TO DO WITH this?" she began to cry.

"JUST DO WHAT THE FUCK WE SAID," J.R. REPLIED, PULLING the gun from his waist.

THE TWO OF THEM WATCHED AS SHE STRUGGLED TO DIAL the number.

"PUT IT ON SPEAKER!" COREY DEMANDED AND SHE did as she was told.

THE PHONE RANG A FEW TIMES BEFORE A MALE'S VOICE finally answered.

TWYLA T.

"I'M BUSY RIGHT NOW MA, LET ME CALL YOU BACK....."

"NO. NO. NO. LARRY, THERE ARE SOME MEN HERE LOOKING for you and....."

BANG!

J.R. LET OFF ONE SHOT, HITTING LARRY'S MOM DIRECTLY IN between her eyes. He could hear Larry's frantic voice yelling from the other end. Stepping over his lifeless mom's body, J.R. picked up the phone and smiled as if the person on the other end could see him.

"WHAT UP UNC?!" J.R. GRINNED INTO THE PHONE BEFORE looking over at Corey who had a look of approval on his face.

"WHO THE FUCK IS THIS?" LARRY YELLED INTO the phone.

"SO, YOU THOUGHT CUZ YO OG LIVED MILES AWAY, WE wouldn't be able to find her?" J.R. laughed.

"BITCH YO WHOLE FAMILY IS DEAD!" LARRY screamed so loud that J.R. had to move the phone further from his ear.

"YOU SEE OLD HEAD, THIS IS CHESS, NOT CHECKERS. HOW long did you honestly think we was just gon' stand still like some hoes?" J.R. asked into the receiver.

"FUCK YOUUUUU!" LARRY'S ANGRY VOICE SOUNDED but his anger had no effect on either Corey or J.R.

"NOW HOW YOU WANNA DO THIS? WE CAN KEEP PLAYING this cat and mouse game or we can shoot shit up like big boys, but the choice is yours." J.R. replied calmly.

"FUCK YOU. I'LL SEE YOU AROUND."

THE LINE WENT DEAD AND BOTH J.R. AND COREY KNEW exactly what that meant. Although the other leads they got from Jessica turned out unsuccessful, hearing about Larry's estranged mom was like a prize gift for them. The Rock Boyz knew that Larry was going to come for them full force now. J.R. just simply prayed that they were ready.

❧ 26 ❧

hile J.R. and Corey were out of town handling business, Mari and his twin were on the East Side of the A preparing to fuck up some shit. They had part of the team already in motion while they waited for the perfect time to make their move. It wasn't that they needed money or no shit like that, but to them it was all about respect. For someone to steal their shit and then sell it without even having the *decency* to discard their bags and use their own shit didn't sit well with either of the Rock Boyz. When the guys decided to put TRB on each baggie they possessed, it was a way of letting people know who had the quality shit and where to find it. Yeah, they were on some *American Gangster* type shit and it paid off in a major way.

Mari ended the call on the burner phone he was on and placed it in the cup holder. He had to follow up with one of the cops they had on payroll and let him know what was going on before they made a move and was glad that he had gotten it out of the way. They had achieved so much in so little time, but none of it had come easy. Even with the loss that they had taken, money was still good but nobody wanted to lose shit, especially when it came at the hands of a thief. Another text came through on the burner and Mari read it and placed it down once again.

"You ready bruh?" he queried.

"Born ready," Mani replied and Mari put the car in gear and headed towards their destination.

It wasn't even noon, but that didn't matter to either one of the Rock Boyz. They were on a mission and had a statement to make. As Mari drove, he noticed that his twin seemed a little frustrated with something. He contemplated asking him what the problem was, but knew that he really needed to stay focused. When Mani sighed, he said *fuck it* and decided to see what was up.

"The hell wrong wit you man?"

"Just some bullshit I gotta handle. Ion even wanna talk about it right now, let's go fuck these niggaz up," Mani responded.

"Say less," Mari's mind went right back to the business.

Fifteen minutes later, Mari parked and killed the engine. One of the youngsters had already informed them that the lil leader of the East Side crew was inside, and that was all they needed to hear. Mari and Mani got out and walked up the street like they owned it. Once they made it to the door, they pulled their guns and walked in with the exact same authority they had possessed while walking down the street.

"Don't fuckin' move!!" Mani based.

"Who the fuck y..."

Before dude could finish his sentence or retrieve the gun that he was going for, Mari sent one shot to his heart and laid him down, permanently.

"Anybody else ready to die before time?" Mari asked.

Silence filled the room, but if looks could kill, Mari and Mani would be some dead muthafuckas. He studied the room and was disgusted at each person that he saw. When his eyes got to one of their workers, he noticed the leader of the crew and nothing but fear was etched on his face. The game that they were in, fear wasn't a quality to possess. Mari walked his way and he saw Mani taking slow steps out of his peripheral.

"You working for that fat fuck nigga they call Larry?" Mari quizzed when he got close to him.

"Man we sold all y'all shit, but I got triple for it. Just let me go in the back and get the money," the guy squealed.

Mari couldn't help but to think about how much of a bitch that nigga was and he shook his head.

"Lead, I'll follow... and if you try any stupid shit my niggaz out in Douglasville won't hesitate to gun up in that brick house with the red Impala and white Silverado that's out front," Mari spat, letting him know that he knew where his people resided.

"Man I just want my life... I swear to God y'all can have it all."

Mari followed him to the back room and was confident that Mani and the other workers had everything on lock in the front. He looked on as dude unlocked the safe and money started falling out. He thought to himself that those niggaz were stupid as fuck to keep that much money in one spot.

"Put it in bags," D'Mari instructed.

It took the guy all of five minutes to stuff the money in a two duffle bags. As soon as Mari had the money in his possession, he sent a bullet right between ol' buddy's eyes. Right on cue, shots rang out in the front and Mari knew that no one but the Rock Boyz were left standing. He walked back to the front with a bag on each arm and smiled at the fellas.

"That was the easiest got damn money we done made all year. Let's go do this one more time and get the fuck home," he told the crew.

❦ 27 ❦

After finding out that there was a chance Imani belonged to someone else, D'Mani was more than pissed, but there was still work that needed to be put in. They were still waiting on some type of retaliation after killing Larry's mama and hitting his trap. The way that nigga had been moving, D'Mani knew that he needed to be on high alert, ready for whatever he might bring their way. He could breathe a little better knowing that the kids were all safe but the sisters being there made it difficult for him to be fully focused.

It was a bunch of shit on his mind and he hated that once they were done handling business, the main thing he thought about was Imani *not* being his. He hadn't been able to go get a DNA test done immediately after finding out like he wanted to because their business and safety came first. Since they didn't have anything on the agenda that day, he was going to head over to the testing facility that he'd checked out. They told him he could get the results within two to three days; he'd just have to pay a bit extra but that was fine with him. Money was no object when it came to peace of mind.

D'Mani grabbed Imani's little princess brush and checked it to make sure there was hair inside. He had initially been worried that he'd have to wait until she returned from Mississippi, and since they weren't sure when they would catch Larry, there was no telling when that would be. Thankfully, they'd assured him that the test could be done with her hair, but just in case, he would go to Cheyanne's and see if she had an old toothbrush laying around.

He snuck away from the house while everyone was preoccupied so that he wouldn't have to answer any questions about where he was going. After all the times that he'd been asked about Imani's paternity and he always claimed her as his own, it was slightly embarrassing for him to admit that he may have jumped the gun.

The drive over to Cheyanne's was quiet. Not even the radio would have been able to drown out his thoughts anyway. D'Mani wasn't ready to deal with the possibility that he had gone through all of the shit he had with Cheyanne and Anastasia when he didn't have to. And even if Imani wasn't his, what type of man would he be to turn his back on her after she grown used to his family and him? He didn't even know how he would feel if he found out she wasn't his daughter, but he still hoped that she was though.

He pulled into the driveway of her house about thirty minutes later and checked his surroundings before exiting the car. It didn't look like he was followed but after all of the near death experiences they'd all faced, he wasn't trying to take that chance.

With the house keys in hand, he hurried to the door and unlocked it, stepping inside of the dark hall. It was crazy how not too long ago that same house was filled with people celebrating Imani's birthday and now it seemed abandoned. D'Mani really didn't have time to be thinking about that though and he quickly shook off the depressing thoughts and headed up the stairs, hitting each light on the way. He didn't care how quiet it seemed, the life they lived kept him paranoid. Imani's room was the first one once he reached the landing. Luckily for him, she still had a toothbrush inside of her tiny bathroom and then he headed to Cheyanne's room next to grab something of hers. He didn't know much about DNA tests, but he knew that he would need a sample from the mother as well. Her personal things were still out on the dresser, the exact same way that she'd left them when she was there last. He snatched up her comb and brush since he hadn't thought to at their house and was on his way down the stairs when pounding at the door froze him in place. D'Mani put the items in his hands down into his pockets and crept to the door. His first thought was that it was Stasia, which was why he didn't immediately pull out his gun. He may not have thought he was followed but those damn sisters stayed in some shit. It wouldn't be farfetched for them to have trailed him, thinking he was up to no good. Through the peephole though, he was able to see that it was Cheyanne's mama standing on the other side of the door with her face twisted into a deep scowl.

Running a hand down his face, he slowly opened the door and her eyes widened in surprise before she squinted suspiciously.

"Where is Cheyanne and what you doin' answering her door?" she questioned, pushing her way inside and looking around. D'Mani didn't know what to say. He knew that she didn't really fuck with her mama, but he didn't think that she had left her in the dark about what was going on with her health. He attempted to think of how he could tell her that her daughter was dead while she stormed through each room on the lower level talking shit.

He finally snapped out of it when she came back from checking the kitchen and was headed up the stairs. Grabbing her hand as she reached the second step, he stopped her from continuing.

"Cheyanne... she... died. She had a... a heart problem," he told her, and she looked at him like he had shit on his forehead before snatching away and clutching her chest.

"You a goddamn lie! She would have told me if she was sick! What the fuck are you even talking about?! And where is Imani?" She turned on him quickly, gripping her worn brown purse like she was about to hit him with it.

"Listen, she must didn't want you to know.... She only recently told me," He tried to explain, but she wasn't having it.

"I don't believe that shit!" She continued in irritation. "What the fuck you do to my baby huh? She was just fine before yo ass came around, now all of a sudden she had a heart problem! Don't think I don't know what type of shit you into! You reek of drug dealer! If she died, it was because of you! Now where is my grand baby? I know Cheyanne wouldn't want you raising her!" D'Mani released a deep sigh. He wasn't even expecting to run into anybody on that stop and he ended up having to deal with Cheyanne's dumb ass mama, causing unnecessary stress on top of the stress he was already experiencing. He was trying to be cool, but if she came out of her face with some more bullshit, he was going to forget that she was Imani's grandma.

"I'm sorry for yo loss, but you ain't bouta be talkin' to me like that, and as far as Imani goes, I *know* Chey wants me to have her since she basically told me that and Imani's staying with me!"

"Hmph! Well you can best believe I'll be seeing about that! I know good and god damn well that dumb ass girl ain't leave you with her house and baby! If anybody entitled to stay here and raise Imani, it's me!"

D'Mani was done with the conversation at that point ,and he could understand why Cheyanne had told him that she wanted Imani to stay with him in the letter. Her mama was crazy and money hungry as fuck! Cheyanne had told him she invited her mom and a couple other family members to Imani's party as a peace offering, but the next day, shit went left again and she was tired of the back and forth. He couldn't see how she had gotten that he was taking over the house from what he'd said. There was no reason to believe that anyone was getting the girl's house at all. D'Mani couldn't help but to think about how crazy some people could be, family or not. He had cut a few family members off so he understood Cheyanne's position.

"You gotta get yo disrespectful old ass up outta here!" He shook his head and led her back out onto the porch by the arm while she ranted and raved about her rights. If he could, D'Mani would have called up Aunt Shirley to beat her ass for doing all that extra shit.

"My lawyer will be in touch!" she managed to get out as he slammed the door in her face angrily. He was happy to see her leave without showing her ass over there. He didn't want somebody to call the police and draw any unnecessary attention to him.

D'Mani watched her pull away from the house before he went into the kitchen to get some plastic bags. He hoped them being in his pocket hadn't messed anything up because he wasn't trying to have to dwell on the situation for long, especially with Cheyanne's mama around. She hadn't shed one tear about Cheyanne dying and had immediately started putting claims to her house and daughter like she hadn't even lost anybody. No wonder Cheyanne and Imani were "alone" out there. That brief interaction with her had just taken away some of his anger at Cheyanne for lying to him; but now, he was more determined than ever to find out whether or not Imani was his. That would at least make it easier to gain custody of her over her grandma. Placing everything into separate baggies, he left the house and locked up, heading straight to the testing facility.

28

Corey cruised the streets of Atlanta on his way to check on the new trap houses. Since the Rock Boyz brought Larry's mother life to an end and shut down their trap houses days prior, they decided to shut down their old traps and set up shop in other parts of West Atlanta. Now that the roles were reversed, they knew Larry's vendetta against them was no longer just on a business level. It had turned personal and all they could do was be prepared for whatever he had in store for them.

He pulled up to the trap in Adams Park and killed the engine. Corey observed the traffic flow that the trap was getting and nodded his head in approval. The old trap spots did well but the new location was popping. He hopped out the car, making his way inside where he saw the loyal soldiers working hard to bag the product and counting the money. As he examined the trap, Corey only hoped that their remaining soldiers were solid and not on some fuck shit like the other niggas they had to lay to rest. Satisfied with the way things were flowing, Corey hopped back in his truck and went to check on the other three traps.

After cussing two of the workers out for literally sleeping on the job, Corey slammed the door shut as he left. As he made his way to his truck, his cell phone began ringing in his pocket and he knew it was Alyssa by the ringtone. Hopping behind the wheel, Corey answered his phone.

"Hey bae. Wassup?"

"Baby, I just wanted to let you know that we're about to leave for Mississippi."

"Aight. Y'all be safe and let me know when you make it."

"Okay baby. I can't wait to see our baby girl. I miss her so much."

"Shit, I do too. I can't wait until this shit is over," he started the engine and pulled off down the block.

"Who you telling."

"It will be over soon, bae. I promise."

"Aight Corey," Lyssa spoke sternly. "I'll text you to let you know when we make it or if anything happens."

"Aight baby. I love you."

"I love you too."

Ending the call, Corey was headed towards the highway when another call came through. Not recognizing the number, he declined the call only for the same number to call back again seconds later.

"Hello?" he answered annoyed.

"Is this Corey Washington?"

"Yeah. Who's this?"

"I'm operator number 23 calling to inform that a fire was reported at your home on Yancy Street. The fire department has been dispatched to the property," the woman stated.

"Shit!" he yelled, ending the call and tossing his phone in the passenger's seat.

Corey's speed increased from fifty to eighty in the matter of seconds as he rushed down the highway to his crib. As he got closer to his house, he saw the clouds of black smoke before smelling it in the air. Coming to a screeching halt, Corey hopped out the car and watched as the fire department sprayed the blazing fire with the hoses. With his mouth gapped opened, all he could do was shake his head in disbelief. It didn't take him long to figure out that Larry had to be behind the shit and he was heated. In search of his phone, Corey opened the passenger's door, snatching it out of the seat. Before he called anyone, he had an incoming call from Mari.

"Yo bro."

"Yo! I just got to the fucking mansion and it fucked up from the inside out!"

"What the fuck you mean?"

"Them motherfuckas shot the fucking crib up and fucked up everything in this bitch. I think they were looking for the girls because nothing of value is missing!" Mari shouted.

"They hit the fucking mansion too!"

"What else they hit?"

"Them niggas set my fucking crib on fire! I'm standing here now watching the damn fire department put this shit out!"

"Yo let me call you back. That's J.R."

"Aight."

Corey called Mani to let him know what was going on and before Corey could get a world out, his cousin told him that his house was set on fire. After telling him about his crib and what happened at the mansion, Mani told him he would call him back. Stuffing the phone in his pocket, he noticed the small crowd that gathered outside to watch the firemen extinguish the remaining of the flames. After the fire chief told Corey that his house was set on fire from the outside, he handed him a copy of the report for insurance purposes before they left. Taking another long look at his house, he hopped inside his truck and went to the mansion where he saw J.R. and Mari's cars parked in the driveway. Killing the engine, Corey observed the house from the outside and noticed that the windows on the first floor were shattered and the outside décor was damaged. Before making his way inside, Mani pulled up with screeching tires and jumped out the car. Mani and Corey observed how fucked up the downstairs was. The electronics were broken and the furniture was destroyed. Before either of them could say a word, Mari made his way downstairs with suitcases in his hands.

"Just pack y'all shit. I made a few calls and all this shit will be fixed over the next couple of days," he spoke. "I booked us a few rooms at the Embassy Suites Hotel not too far from here."

"How the fuck did he find us?" Corey questioned.

"That question has a few answers to it but this will be *the last* time he find us."

"I'm tired of this cat and mouse shit bro. It's time for this fat motherfucka to meet his maker. I'm through playing games with this nigga!" Mani shouted.

"I feel you bro," J.R. came from the basement smoking a blunt. "This nigga will fall soon enough."

Corey headed upstairs to his room that was a wreck as well. Grabbing suitcases, he packed all of their things and double checked to make sure he had everything. Making his way downstairs, he put the luggage in the trunk of his car and waited for his brothers to come out of the house. As he examined the outside of the house again, Corey thanked God that the girls weren't inside the house when the mansion was attacked. Just thinking about his wife and sisters being hurt, kidnapped, or killed had him seeing red. That nigga Larry had the upper hand throughout the majority of their beef and it was time for his reign to end.

29

♫ H onestly, I'm tryna stay focused
        You must think I've got to be joking when
        I say
I don't think I can wait
I just need it now
Better swing my way
I just need some dick
I just need some love
Tired of fucking with these lame niggas baby
I just need a thug ♫

The Holiday sisters plus Aunt Shirley sang Summer Walker's new song *"Girls Need Love"* at the top of their lungs. Lexi had a special liking for the song since she hadn't been getting dick'd down like she was used to. Even after her six weeks was up, her and J.R. still didn't have sex like they used to have. She was either sleep when he came in at night or they were too busy arguing to be turned on. She couldn't wait for everything to go back to normal, which she prayed happened soon.

"I can't wait to see my babies," Drea squealed from the driver's seat as they hit the road, heading to Mississippi.

"Girl, me either. My baby probably doesn't even know who I am. I'm a dead beat and so is my baby daddy," Lexi replied sadly.

Although she really felt that way, she stood by her decision to leave her son with her mother. Yasmine was there to help out and Amir loved his Aunt, so she was sure that he was in the right hands.

"I just want all this shit to be over so I can get back to living a normal life," Stasia confessed from the back seat.

"Well since we all talking about our wants and needs... I NEED for y'all to drop me off in Augusta so I can handle some business," Aunt Shirley requested.

"Augusta? FOR WHAT?!" Lyssa quizzed.

"Just know I need to make a stop so put it in ya PGS and get me there."

"It's GPS auntie," Stasia corrected her, making everyone laugh at Shirley's expense.

"A-B-C-D-E-F-G..... I don't give a damn, just get me there," she fussed, grabbing her flask and tossing it back.

"We not making no extra stops. We told our husbands that we'll be in Mississippi at a certain time and we plan on keeping it that way," Drea explained to her.

"Them niggas not my man, I don't give a fuck what y'all told them," Shirley snapped.

"Ok look. We need to eat. Maybe we can grab something while we there," Lexi chimed in.

"Where? Augusta is out of our way. That's stupid," Lyssa hissed from the back.

"You stupid and if yo crackhead ass husband knew how to fight, we wouldn't even be having this discussion," their Auntie explained.

"Fight? What does Corey have to do with this and for the last time, HE IS NOT A CRACKHEAD!" Lyssa yelled.

"Whoa... Whoa... Whoa.... Pull over, I'm about to beat this bitch ass. Who she hollering at?"

Lexi turned around towards the backseat where she peeped Aunt Shirley taking off her jacket. What really tickled Lexi was when her favorite Aunt pulled the little hair she had on her head in a ponytail. She then began taking off the old pearl earrings she wore all the time.

"Calm down Auntie," Lexi giggled as she tried her hardest to be serious.

"Nah, she got me fuck'd up. Like I said, if Corey knew how to fight, he wouldn't have gotten kidnapped, and I wouldn't be asking you hoes for no favor."

"Ok but seriously, why do you want us to stop?" Drea asked.

"It's my man. He needs me."

"Your man?" Stasia smirked.

"When this happen?" Lyssa laughed.

"If y'all must know all my business. I met him on Tinder and...."

"TINDER!" all four sisters repeated aloud before erupting in laughter.

Shirley sat in the backseat with her arms folded across her chest. Lexi knew her aunt played a lot, but she could tell she was serious this time.

"Ok. Ok. Ok. Listen y'all. I don't see any harm in grabbing something to eat or shopping while my TT get her some dicc-ckkkk," Lexi said, dancing in the front seat.

"I mean, she has been running around and dealing with us and our men," Drea sighed deeply from the wheel.

"Not you too Andrea," Stasia replied, shaking her head.

"What would it hurt?" Lexi turned around and asked.

Lexi glanced at Shirley who was busy sticking up her middle finger at Lyssa and Stasia. The group had made up their mind to allow her some time to do her thang. Figuring it was harmless, they headed to Augusta before making their way back home.

Lexi grabbed her headphones and plugged them up when a text message came through. Seeing Shirley's name on the screen of her phone automatically made Lexi chuckle. Using her thumb print to unlock the iPhone, Lexi went directly to her text messages.

Favorite Auntie: You see how these bitches be hating on me. Drea cool when she wanna be but them other two hoes.... We might have to fuck them up!

Laughing out loud caused everyone in the car to look at Lexi crazy but she remained silent.

"So, Auntie, who is this man?" Lyssa asked, nudging Stasia with her elbow.

"Why? He don't want you," she smacked her lips.

"I damn sholl don't want him," Lyssa replied, rolling her neck and eyes playfully.

"Right. You always in our business, we figured we would get in yours," Stasia replied.

Aunt Shirley and the Holiday sisters argued the few hours it took for them to get from Atlanta to Augusta. Lexi tuned them out with the trap music that blasted through her headphones. She was ready to grab something to eat and stretch her legs.

"My baby said he meeting us at The Juicy Crab. He says it's a seafood restaurant on Washington," Aunt Shirley cleared her throat and announced.

"I can definitely go for some seafood," Lexi beamed.

"Ohhh me too!" Lyssa agreed excitedly.

"So cool. Aunt Shirley, meet us back here at seven, that way, we can still make it to Mississippi at a reasonable time," Drea stated and Aunt Shirley agreed.

❧ 30 ❧

"**S**ooo since we got a few hours away from Aunt Shirley, we can spend some quality time together before we get back to our babies," Drea beamed.

"One of y'all gotta smoke wit me while my auntie gone," Lexi said.

"Weed makes me paranoid sister, that's the only reason I won't smoke wit ya," Stasia replied.

"Welp, solo it is. I know those other two hoes ain't gon' do shit," Lexi rolled her eyes.

"You're right Alexis... so how about we go this spa and get their full service," Drea mentioned as she scrolled through her phone.

"That's cool wit me," Stasia replied.

"I'm wit it," Lexi chimed in.

"That's fine," Lyssa agreed last.

"Well let's go," Drea gathered her stuff and prepared to leave.

The waitress dropped the ticket off and never came back, but they left a tip anyway and Drea walked to the register so she could pay for their food. A lady walked up and asked what they had without making eye contact. Drea shook her head, but proceeded with handing her a hundred dollar bill along with the receipt. Once the lady was done, she slid Drea's change to her, and Drea just stood there.

"Uh oh... this bitch bout to make this girl go to jail," Lexi appeared and said.

"Umm do you need something else?" the lady finally made eye contact and asked.

"Umm yeah, I need you to hand me my money like I handed it to you," Drea matched her tone.

The lady turned red as a stop sign, but Drea didn't back down.

"If we were nice enough to patronize this restaurant, then I need y'all to be nice enough to respect us."

By the time she was done talking, her change had been placed in her outstretched hand and Lexi ran off. Drea didn't know where she went until she walked back up with money in her hands. She knew then that she had went and retrieved the tip money that they had left. The sisters exited the mom and pop seafood restaurant without looking back.

"Drea, you need some of this blunt now for real," Lexi entreated, in which Drea ignored her ass.

According to the GPS, the Serenity Massages & Wellness Spa was less than two miles away. Silently, Stasia had become the main driver and if she didn't complain, the sisters wouldn't say shit either. They pulled up to the spa and Lexi immediately began fussing because she wasn't able to finish her blunt.

"Save that shit for later and come on," Drea hissed and got out.

She heard Lexi mumbling under her breath, but she ignored her and went on inside. They didn't have any reservations, so she was anxious to see if they could all get treatment. Upon entrance, Drea was greeted and she smiled. That made her happy because the incident at the restaurant had her ready to get the hell out of Augusta.

"Do you all have room for four within the next few minutes for full service?" Drea quizzed after speaking.

"As a matter of fact, we do. Is this your first time with us?"

"It is," Drea replied as the door chimed. She heard her sisters without even having to look.

"We're going to make this very special for you lovely ladies, and I'll also throw in our twenty-five percent off discount," the girl smiled.

"Thank you so much... I'll be taking care of the ticket," Drea grabbed her debit card out of her wallet and handed it to the girl.

The sisters were led to the back and given robes and slippers to put on. A few moments later, they were given Mimosas and snacks. Even though they had just eaten, it didn't stop them from being greedy and grabbing a few things. They were instructed to chill for a few minutes and then the pampering would begin.

"Do y'all ever just sit back and think about how far we've come and how blessed we are?" Drea asked once all of them were seated and relaxed.

"I know I do. I can't believe how much we used to fuss at each other, but I'm glad we're all close now," Alyssa spoke up first, shocking everyone.

"Dammnnn Lyssa, yo whiny ass always the last to agree but the first to say *I do know*, Lexi laughed.

"See, you always talking shit."

"Well, she is right Lyssa," Stasia said before Drea did.

"On some real shit, we still petty as fuck and gon' be petty forever, but I'm glad we close and shit. We really are blessed. Who else y'all know can leave a bunch of newborn babies with their moms and shit?" Lexi pointed out and they all agreed.

"Speaking of babies... I never asked this, but Drea... why yo ass didn't even tell nobody you was pregnant... well Lexi probably knew, but we didn't and I thought we wasn't keeping anymore secrets," Stasia queried.

"Shit I really didn't know... remember I was drinking and shit? My OB said it was probably because I switched pills. Mari wants more kids, but I'm really good. I won't deny him, but I ain't tryna convince him either. The twins are enough. You gon' give Mani a baby though?"

"Yeah hoe... what you waiting on?"

"Wellll... it's not like we needed to bring a kid in the mix of all this drama. He have Imani now anyway, so I'm good unless he brings it up," Stasia shrugged.

The sisters transitioned to a room to get facials, then a full body massage, and they ended with manis and pedis. Four hours had passed before they knew it and they only had another hour or so left before it was time to pick up Aunt Shirley and head back to Mississippi. They hit up a couple of stores and cracked jokes the entire time, doing typical Holiday sister shit.

The sisters had a nice time at the spa and shopping, and all Anastasia wanted to do was grab their Aunt and head to Mississippi so that she could see the kids and rest. She was beginning to consider Imani just as much her child as Kyler and she knew that was what D'Mani had been hoping for all along. Anastasia didn't want to say that it was because her mother was no longer around, but it was precisely for that reason. As terrible as it may sound with Cheyanne there, she didn't feel as if she had a role in Imani's life. She cared for her, but she was constantly worried about overstepping boundaries when it came to her position as D'Mani's significant other. As a mother herself, she knew that she would hate it if a bitch tried to come in and play mama to her baby. Even though she highly disliked her earlier on, she wasn't trying to seem like one of them girlfriends to Cheyanne. The problem now was D'Mani. Although he seemed okay, she knew that something had to be bothering him. She tried to be patient and extra supportive so that he would feel comfortable telling her, but that wasn't working. It could have been what they had going on in the streets but she knew it wasn't. The last time he'd been acting all strange with her was when he had found out about Imani, and she really wanted to give him the benefit of doubt. But if another "ex" popped up with a baby, she was going to kill him. Literally.

"Ummm, where the hell this old bird at?" Drea questioned, breaking her out of her thoughts. Anastasia looked up and realized that they were back at the restaurant, but Aunt Shirley was nowhere in sight. She checked the time on her phone to make sure they weren't too early and realized that they were right on time.

"Maybe she's inside waiting." Alyssa shrugged.

"Or maybe she still getting that diiiiiick!" Lexi stuck her tongue out and danced in the front seat, causing her sisters to groan.

"Ugh, bitch! Kill the visual!" Stasia covered her face with her hands, but still had to squeeze her eyes closed to stop the burning she suddenly felt in them.

"Don't do my Aunty!"

"Girl, ain't nobody tryna think about Aunt Shirley fuckin'," Andrea said dryly. None of them wanted to have that thought in their heads.

"I'ma go check and see if she in there," Alyssa got out quickly and disappeared behind the glass door of the restaurant.

"Y'all some haters," Lexi huffed, rolling her eyes.

"Whatever! Why don't you try calling your favorite Aunty and see where her ass at cause we don't got time for this. We need to get on the road," Drea huffed before looking around the parking lot again. Lexi mumbled a *fine* and pulled her phone out.

"She not answering," she shrugged.

"Let me try." Anastasia put in the code to her phone and searched through her contacts for her Aunt's number.

"If she ain't answer for her favorite niece, what make you

think she gone answer for yo ass?" Anastasia rolled her eyes at her sister and went to dial up their Aunt. The phone went straight to voicemail just as Alyssa came out of the restaurant and shrugged her shoulders.

"Where the hell she at?" Drea sighed and looked at the time again, growing more frustrated. They weren't even supposed to be stopping anyway and now Aunt Shirley was about to fuck some shit up being late.

"Y'all don't think nothing happened to her do y'all?" Lyssa slid into the car and asked. The sisters all looked at each other, hoping that their Aunty was safe and only running late. That thought quickly started to fade when she still hadn't shown up an hour later.

"I told y'all--"

"If it's taking this long to get some dick, her ass dead Alexis!" Drea cut her sister off, already knowing what she was about to say. "We just gone have to get a room for the night cause it's about to be late, and this seat getting uncomfortable as hell."

"Yeah let's gone 'head get a room cause I'm tired of sitting out here too," Stasia said. She was tired and already hungry again after the day's events. They had already tried calling their Aunt repeatedly and they still hadn't gotten an answer.

"What if she come while we gone though?" Alyssa pointed out.

"Well she better charge her phone then so she can call us." It was clear that Lexi was beginning to get tired of the waiting herself.

"Okay well we agree we'll go get a room and just keep on trying to reach her," Drea said and they all nodded. Stasia hoped that everything was okay and that their Aunt was just being careless as usual. The last thing that they needed was for her to be in some kind of trouble, considering that the men were currently into some shit and the fact that they were supposed to be in Mississippi by then. She dialed up her phone three more times, still getting the voicemail as her sister headed toward the closest hotel. Setting her phone aside, Stasia blew out a deep breath, feeling as though this detour wasn't such a good idea. If Shirley didn't show up or call back soon, they would be forced to call the men and that was the last thing they wanted to have to do.

❧ 32 ❧

After checking into the Holiday Inn, the sisters continued to take turns calling Aunt Shirley, but they all kept getting her voicemail. Their emotions went from being frustrated to worried and they were all hoping that their aunt would turn up soon, so they could hit the road and go home. It had been a while since they saw their kids and they were anxious to get back home to see them. Every time Victoria sent her a new picture of her baby girl Alana, Alyssa couldn't stop herself from crying. Her daughter was growing up without her and she was tired of being so far away from her baby.

As much as Aunt Shirley got on their nerves, neither of them wanted to assume the worse but her lack of consideration for them was pissing Alyssa off the most. It took two seconds to shoot a text or to pick up the phone to let them know she was alright, but the fact that they haven't heard from their aunt in hours made Alyssa start to panic a little bit.

As it got later in the evening, the Holiday sisters sat in

silence as they watched TV, waiting for their phones to ring.
Lost in their own thoughts, Alyssa couldn't help but to think
about her husband and how he was going to react if he knew
they were in Augusta instead of Mississippi. Thinking back to
when they left Mississippi to search for Corey, Alyssa
chuckled to herself about how their sneaky asses managed to
maneuver around the city without getting caught until they
had to stop to feed their aunt. Even though Aunt Shirley was
always in the way and she kept calling her husband a
crackhead, Alyssa and the rest of her sisters loved their crazy
ass auntie and she hoped that Aunt Shirley just lost track of
time and not in any danger.

Minutes later, Drea's phone rang, causing everyone to
look in her direction in hopes it was Aunt Shirley, but when
she announced it was their mother, they all sighed.

"We shoulda known that wasn't Aunt Shirley," Stasia
stated dryly. "If she was gonna call anybody, it would be Lexi."

"You're right about that," Lyssa replied.

"She must be getting the best dick of her life for her to
just say fuck us," Lexi huffed.

"Shhhh y'all," Drea silenced them, covering the phone.

The three of them remained silent until Drea got off the
phone with their mom minutes later.

"Wassup Drea? What mommy talking about?" Lexi sat up
the table, pulling out her weed to roll up.

"She wanted to know what was taking us so long. I told
her we got tired of driving and well be there sometime
tomorrow," she sighed. "Leave it to Aunt Shirley to fuck up
the plans yet again."

"Wayment. When was the last time my auntie fucked up
our plans?" Lexi jumped in.

"She's the reason why we got caught when we were
looking for Corey with her greedy ass," Lyssa rolled her eyes.

"Why you bringing up old shit Lyssa?"

"I'm just saying. It seems like every time we make a pit stop for her ass, we end up getting caught and cussed out by our niggas," Stasia chimed in.

"Y'all gonna stop blaming my auntie for shit," Lexi defended her.

"Cut the bullshit Lexi. You know we're telling the truth," Lyssa dismissed her with a hand wave.

"Aight y'all. Cool out," Drea interfered. "None of that matters now. We stopped so auntie could spend time with her dude. Neither of us thought that she was going to jam us like this but she did. It's fifteen minutes to eight and we still haven't heard from her. Our men don't know where we are and we don't know if something happened to our aunt."

"So what are you saying, Drea?" Stasia asked.

"I'm saying....we're gonna have to call our men and tell them what's going on," she answered in annoyance. "So, who's gonna be the first one to call?"

They looked at each other with wide eyes and when their eyes landed on Lexi, she shook her head.

"Y'all got me fucked up. I'm not calling J.R. to tell him this bullshit," she finished rolling her blunt.

"Aunt Shirley is ya favorite aunt and ya ass basically co-signed us stopping here," Stasia stated.

"I don't give a fuck about none of that. I'll call him but I'm not calling him first," Lexi stood to her feet. "Now y'all figure this shit out while I go smoke," she headed out the room, slamming the door shut.

"So, who's gonna make the call?" Drea looked between Lyssa and Stasia.

When Alyssa noticed four eyes on her, she let out a sigh of frustration before grabbing her phone to call her husband. Knowing that she was about to get cussed out yet again because of their aunt, all she could do was brace herself for it and take that shit on the chin.

"From here on out, if we gotta make moves, Aunt Shirley can no longer be apart of our missions. She better keep her drunk ass in Mississippi," Alyssa huffed as she waited for her husband to answer his phone.

❧ 33 ❧

"**S**o, my homie Goo said that nigga hadn't even been back to the city since we laid his OG down. His auntie been handling shit, but the funeral is scheduled for this weekend. I say we air that mu'fucka out," J.R. told the guys while they were sitting at one of the local bars drinking.

"You really wanna shoot up the funeral?" Corey asked.

"Hell fuckin' yeah! I'm tired of playing around with this pussy ass nigga! We need to kill this nigga and take a fuckin' vacation then get back to the money," J.R. replied.

"I think we all ready to kill that nigga, but too many innocent people gonna be at the funeral. Let's trail that nigga and hit him when he leave the cemetery or some shit," Mari suggested.

"I don't care which one we do... funeral, cemetery, that nigga needs to be put to rest wit his mama this weekend," Mani fumed.

They sat around taking shots, talking shit, and discussing business. Corey's phone rang and all of the guys' eyes went to him when he raised his voice at Alyssa. He talked to her for a few minutes and the rest of them impatiently waited to see

163

what was up because all of the women were on the road headed back to Mississippi.

"Are you fuckin' serious?" Mari questioned after Corey told them what Alyssa said.

"As a heart attack," Corey responded.

"You know they not gon' leave their aunt either, but it's good they not in Atlanta at least," Corey replied.

"Fuck that! They so fuckin' hard headed. Let me call Drea," Mari said and Mani and J.R. made comments about calling Stasia and Lexi.

When Drea didn't answer, Mari balled his fists and visualized snatching her ass up. He had never put his hands on a woman before, but the way the Holiday sisters weren't taking shit serious, he wanted to snatch all of their asses up. It appeared that all of the men agreed when none of them answered their phones.

"One of us just gon' have to drive their asses to Mississippi y'all. But for now, let's just go on and head to Augusta and make sure they straight and find Aunt Shirley. I ain't gon' be able to rest if they're not with us or out of this state," Mari explained.

The guys paid their tabs and headed out. The hotel they were staying at wasn't far away, but Mari didn't wanna waste any extra time, so he told Corey that him and J.R. could get their cars later. They had all been out in different directions and decided to meet up at the bar about an hour ago. Once they were all situated in the truck, Mari headed out, speeding heavily as they made the two hour drive to find their women, calling their women constantly without no response. Jeezy's old *Hustlerz Ambition* album filled the truck and J.R. got a backwood in rotation.

"Aunt Shirley do a lot of shit, but she really ain't the type to come up missing. Y'all think she aight?" Corey quizzed, finally cutting into the silence that had taken over. Mari was pushing the hell out of his truck, eating up good time on the highway.

"That old lady got them hands... I'm sure her drunk ass aight," J.R. stated.

"You stupid man, but I ain't gon' lie... she do a lot of shit, but I was slick wondering where the fuck she would just run off too myself. They in fuckin' Augusta, something don't seem right," Mari expressed.

Before anyone could respond, Mari's phone rang and he connected the Bluetooth instantly. They had been on the road for a little over an hour already when he finally heard from his wife.

"Andrea Mitchell!! What the fuck y'all on? Why y'all don't take shit serious? We in the middle of a fuckin' war and y'all keep playing these kiddie games," Mari fussed.

"D'Mari, I'm sorry... I know you don't wanna hear what I got to say, but I do take shit serious and I'm sorry. I'm not even bout to argue with you. We wrong, and Ima leave it at that," Drea replied, shocking the hell outta the whole truck.

Mari figured that her ass must have really been scared and worried because Drea wasn't the type to give in so easily. That in itself made him speed up so that he could get to his wife.

"What hotel y'all going to?"

"The Holiday Inn is the only place we could get, so we'll stay here and leave in the morning," Drea explained.

"Aight... don't y'all go nowhere else Drea. I mean it."

"Okay baby. I love you."

"I love you too," Mari ended the call.

Like clockwork, the other guys' phones rang, but J.R. and Mani went harder on Lexi and Stasia. Mari was shocked that they didn't fuss much either. *We must be wearing their asses down*, he thought to himself.

About thirty minutes later, Mari was turning into the Holiday Inn parking lot. He managed to cut twenty minutes off of the two hour drive. He sent Drea a text and asked what room they were in and she sent the confused emoji, but then texted the number.

"They in room 426 y'all... come on."

The guys piled out of the truck and then made their way inside. It was almost eleven o'clock when Mari looked at the time on his phone. It was too damn late for the girls to get on the road, so they would just head back to Atlanta and someone would drive their asses the next day to ensure they really got there. They went straight to the elevator and Mari hit the four. The doors closed and they headed up, only to stop on the second floor and then the third.

"Damn we coulda took the stairs," Mani fussed as the doors finally closed.

"Where the damn ice machine at?"

"Wait... wasn't that Aunt Shirley's voice?" Mari stated more than asked.

"Damn shol' sounded like her ass," J.R. agreed.

When the elevator reached the fourth floor, Mari hit the three and closed the doors back fast as hell.

"If it was her, how we gon' know where she went?" Mani asked.

"That big ass mouth of hers... we'll hear her from a mile away."

"So what if we do find her... what if she wit a man or some shit? Corey asked and everyone laughed out loud.

"That old woman ain't wit no man... she probably at a hotel party drinking or some shit," J.R. cajoled.

They walked the hall of the third floor and just when Mari was about to give up, he heard *that* voice again.

"Bingo," he said as he stood outside of room 318.

"Wait, you finna knock... the fuck you gon' say?" Mani queried.

"Sound like a party like J.R. said... just watch."

166

Knock knock.

"Who is it? Oh that must be the room service you ordered baby," Aunt Shirley said after a few seconds.

Mari covered the peep hole and planned on snatching her ass up as soon as she opened the door. Instead of Aunt Shirley opening the door, the guys got the shock of their lives and apparently *Larry* did too. As soon as he turned to run, Mari felt a breeze fly by his head and Larry went down. He turned to see Corey's gun in his hand and was happy as fuck that the silencer was on.

"NOOOOO!!" Aunt Shirley screamed as she came out of the bathroom and the guys reacted fast by piling in the room and closing the door. Larry laid on the floor, moaning with a big ass hole in his ass. Rushing over to him, Mani and J.R. picked Larry up off the floor, stuffed a thrown shirt that was laying on the floor in his mouth to muffle his screams, and tied him to a chair that was sitting near the hotel desk. They didn't know what the fuck kinda sex shit that Aunt Shirley and Larry had been engaging in, but they were grateful for the rope and handcuffs that came in handy.

"What the hell y'all doin'? Crackhead, you shot my man before I could get some more dick! Oh my Lord, y'all gonna kill him!" Shirley fussed and sobbed a little.

"Calm down Aunt Shirley and talk quietly. How the fuck you know this nigga? Was he using you to get to us?" Mari asked her.

"Naw...not that I know of. I met him on Tinder... why y'all gonna kill my Georgia meat? Y'all better be glad I don't love his ass or nothing but shit... where my drink? Ain't nobody died that close to me since I ki... never mind... well, he ain't dead yet but soon enough huh? Anyways... where my damn drink... fuck this shit y'all got going on."

While J.R. and Mani were asking Aunt Shirley questions, Mari sent a text to the cleanup crew to get them en route.

Once he was done, the brothers knew what they had to do to get Aunt Shirley to leave so that they could finally and properly deal with Larry's bitch ass once and for all.

"Aunt Shirley... we owe you aight, but don't speak on this... *at all*. We need you to head out to the girls' room while we handle this shit. They're in this hotel...room 426," Mari instructed.

"Aight... but I ain't got time for their shit. I already know that they are going to be fussing and cussing since I've been ignoring their fucking calls. But y'all's secret is safe wit me... I knew I loved y'all asses for a reason, even crackhead ova there," Aunt Shirley smiled as she counted the money that Mari, J.R., and Mani had just handed her and exited the room.

Once Aunt Shirley was gone, the brothers didn't waste any time beating the fuck out of Larry. They took all of their frustrations and angst out on him because he had cause them nothing but unnecessary trouble and drama for months. With a bleeding ass and being tied up, all Larry could do was take the beating because his screams fell on death doors...literally. After the fellas got tired of beating his ass, the brothers watched as Corey stood over Larry's body and emptied his clip, grateful that the silencer was still in place. He had suffered the most at the hands of Larry, so Mari understood and didn't say shit. As he stood there and watched, Mari said fuck it, put his silencer in place and let it rip. Mani and J.R. did the same thing and by the time they were done, Larry's face was unrecognizable.

"Rest in hell you fat muthafucka!" Mari spat after they all were satisfied.

It turned out that the Holiday sisters and their aunt had done more good than harm. Larry was finally a dead muthafucka and their lives could finally go back to normal. No one left the room until the cleanup crew arrived. The brothers took time to freshen up and change clothes to get ensure that Larry's blood wasn't anywhere on them. Mari had also texted the cop on their payroll to pull some strings with camera footage. They had to be sure there was no trace of anything. Around one o'clock, the guys joined the girls in their suite along with Aunt Shirley and told them they had found her at the bar.

❧ 34 ❧

The next morning, Corey was the first one up and ready to hit the road. The satisfaction of bringing Larry's life to an end hours before had him floating on cloud nine. Neither of them thought that Aunt Shirley would be laid up with the nigga that had caused nothing but problems for them for nearly two months. With Larry out of the way, they were all happy that their lives could go back to the way it used to be before all the madness started. Corey was anxious to get to his baby girl so he could love up on her. The last time he saw Alana was the day he was kidnapped and he was missing the hell out of his daughter. Corey was glad that he was back to looking like his handsome self and his body was fully healed because he knew if Alana saw him with his injuries, she would do nothing but cry at the sight of him.

After waking Alyssa up, Corey knocked on his brothers' room doors to make sure they were up. When he got to Aunt Shirley's room, he heard her cussing him out on the other side but instead of telling her to get ready, Corey just let her be—being as though he was the one that brought her man's life to an end. When he got back to the room, Alyssa was tying up her *Air Force Ones*. Doubling checking to make sure they had everything, the couple left the room with their bags in their hand and checked out of the hotel. They tossed their luggage in the trunk and Alyssa hopped in the truck while Corey hopped behind the wheel.

"I can't wait to get to Mississippi," she squealed. "I hope Alana remembers us."

"She will. I'm sure she's gonna be happy to see us," Corey took her hand in his.

"When we come back, will we be going back to the mansion or will we be going home?"

"I'm trying to find us a new house right now, but we might have to stay at a hotel when we get back," he looked at her.

"A new house? What's wrong with our old one?" Confusion laced her voice.

"It was burned down bae."

The couple stared at each other for a moment and he knew by the expression on her face that she was fed up with his current lifestyle.

"I know you're pissed Lyssa but the good thing is that the war is over and we can move on with our lives."

"But what if something like this happens again Corey? I don't wanna have to up and leave again because y'all done got into some shit."

"Believe me when I tell you bae, I will never put you or my daughter through this shit again. I promise," he kissed her hand.

"Cut out all the mushy shit and let's go. You wanna be knocking on my door all early in the morning and shit," Aunt Shirley ranted on her way to the car.

Shaking his head, Corey looked up and saw that the rest of the family were walking out of the hotel heading towards their cars. Lexi and Aunt Shirley drove in the car together while everyone else rode with their spouses. When everyone was ready, he brought the car to life and pulled out of the parking lot with everyone following behind him. The couple talked for the majority of the six hour ride until Alyssa nodded off to sleep. Reminiscing about the past, Corey cringed at the way he was before he went to rehab and what caused him to get there. He never thought that he would be the type to have a drug and alcohol addiction. He never knew how real that shit was until he went through it and was forever grateful that he had a family that cared enough about his ass to make him go to rehab to get himself together. He vowed to take his own life before he put his wife and brothers through that dumb shit again.

Pulling up to the family house, Corey parked before waking up Alyssa. He hopped out the car then walked around to the passenger's side to help his wife out. The family all parked behind each other and everyone climbed out of their cars. Before they could enter the house, Yasmine opened the door with her nephew in her arms. When Lexi saw her baby, she took off running towards the front door, removing her son from Yasmine's arms. Everyone piled inside the house and showed loved to Victoria and Yasmine before finding their kids. Kyler and Imani leaped into their parents' arms, hugging Mani and Stasia tightly. Mari and Drea picked Ava and DJ up out of the pack-n-play and smothered their babies with kisses. Before Corey could ask about Alana, Yasmine spoke up.

"Y'all baby girl is upstairs in your bedroom. Alana has to sleep by herself because the slightest noise wakes her up and if she doesn't sleep for at least an hour, she cries something awful," she chuckled.

While Lyssa thanked Yasmine, Corey ran up the stairs by twos. Opening the door to his wife's room, he saw his baby girl lying in her pack-n-play, staring up at the ceiling. He walked over to her and looked into her bright brown eyes.

Corey's heart broke because he didn't get the smile she always gave him when he saw her, but after a few more seconds, Alana's face lit up. Swooping her up into his arms, Corey gave her a bunch of kisses on her little cheeks.

"I knew you didn't forget about me," he cooed.

Alyssa entered the room seconds later and walked over to where he was standing.

"Oh my goodness! She's so chunky now," she gasped.

"That baby got an appetite like her daddy," Corey smiled at Alana.

With his daughter in his arms, the couple joined the family downstairs and chilled for a few hours. Having the entire family back together again felt like old times. They listened to Victoria and Yasmine tell stories about the kids and the crazy stunts they pulled throughout their stay with their grandmother. They all laughed when his mother-in-law talked about how she went from having one grand baby to five in a short amount of time. Although she looked worn out, Corey could tell that Victoria enjoyed watching the kids. Although he promised Alyssa that this situation wouldn't happen again, he said a prayer to make sure that they wouldn't have to send their women or kids back to Mississippi under these circumstances.

🏵 35 🏵

The sun shined through the blinds, waking D'Mani from a sound sleep. It seemed like he'd been able to rest easier since they'd taken care of Larry's bitch ass. After finally being able to kill the nigga responsible for all of the chaos they'd been going through, they all felt like a vacation was much needed. As soon as they picked up the kids and their ladies, they decided to leave the states. On a whim, Bora Bora came up in conversation and since it was a location none of them had traveled to, they agreed that would be their next stop. Besides the trip though, he had something else special planned for Stasia and he was just waiting on the right moment to spring it on her.

"Hmmm good morning bae," she cooed and snuggled closer to him in the huge California King. Even though he'd kept her up half the night with multiple orgasms, she looked well rested and gorgeous as ever. He planted a light kiss on her forehead and gave her body a squeeze.

"Morning ma, you wanna try and get a quickie in before the kids?"

"Daaaaaadddddyyyy!" Imani called from the other side of the door interrupting him.

"Nope." Stasia smirked and wiggled away. D'Mani released a heavy sigh as he watched her slip on her robe and hurry to open the door for Imani. He couldn't help smiling as they stood there interacting with one another. It was like every time he saw them together, it just made it more and more obvious that he was making the right decision in marrying her. The way her and Imani took to each other was more than he could have hoped for. He'd gotten the results back right before they went and picked them up, proving that Imani was indeed his daughter, but surprisingly, the *only* thing that was different was the relief he felt about not having to tell Stasia that he even needed a test. He realized that as soon as he picked her up that he wouldn't have cared either way; but the fact that she *was* his was one of the strongest defenses he had against Cheyanne's mama besides a letter she'd left with her lawyer for him to get custody once she passed. That was more than enough for a judge to throw out any case Chey's mama tried to come with. Even though he had yet to hear from her, he would still stay ready just in case.

"Can we go get pancakes?" Kyler hopped on the bed and started jumping up and down.

"Pancakes! Pancakes!" Imani shouted, joining him.

"Oh y'all must got some money huh?" D'Mani laughed, not moving from his spot.

"No, you got it." Kyler stopped jumping and shrugged like it was obvious that his ass was paying.

"Duuuuh daddy!" Imani rolled her eyes and put her little hands on her hips.

"Oh, I got it?" D'Mani asked and snatched them both down, tickling them both. They could barely breathe from laughing so hard.

"Ok ok, stop before they pass out," Stasia said after a while.

"Y'all lucky she just came and saved y'all." He let them up and Stasia quickly shooed them out of the room so that they could both get dressed. She closed the door behind them and immediately dropped her robe. Silently, she headed straight to the bathroom and he was right behind her.

An hour later, they were enjoying breakfast inside of their villa and talking about their plans for the day. Of course, D'Mani didn't care what Anastasia thought she was going to be doing because he already had their day mapped out.

"I think we might hit the beach with my sisters and the fellas. I just gotta call and confirm cause plans be changing," she said, stuffing a forkful of pancakes into her mouth. D'Mani just shrugged and nodded. He had already talked to his brothers and her sisters and they all knew what they were supposed to do.

Like clockwork, her phone rang with a call that he knew was coming from Drea. She was supposed to get her out for some shopping while they set things up on the beach for them. He was already prepared when she hung up and looked at him guiltily.

"Do you mind if I go shopping with Drea real quick before we hit the beach?" She wanted to know. "I'll take Imani with because I know they have some cute lil girl clothes out here, and I don't wanna mess up her size."

"Uhhh yeah, me and Ky can get a football game goin' with the fellas," he said over the cheers from the kids. That was even better for him since it would be easier to handle Kyler than Imani when he already had so much to do.

After cleaning Imani up, they headed out the door to meet Drea who's villa was next to theirs. Not even five minutes later, the whole crew invaded their living room with kids in tow.

"Okay let's get this shit over with cause I'm bout tired of y'all hoes getting married out the country!" Aunt Shirley quipped as soon as she set foot inside. They all laughed, used to her antics. "Y'all laughin' and I'm dead ass!" She took a sip from her flask and let out a belch.

"Man what you need us to do?" D'Mari asked, bouncing slightly since he had his baby girl strapped to him with a baby carrier.

"Yeah we don't have much time. Drea ain't gone wanna be out shopping too long," Lexi added, sitting down next to her aunt.

He ended up splitting everyone up to handle different tasks. Since they would all be wearing white, they all had that covered even down to the kids, thanks to Lexi and Alyssa. Mani sent the sisters to get the white roses, JR and Shirley to get the drinks, Corey picked up the rings, and he and D'Mari went to get the pastor.

Once everybody knew what they were going to be doing, they all split up to take care of their job. In the car, he could feel his brother staring a hole into the side of his face.

"What you lookin' at me like that for?" he asked, looking between him and the street.

"I'm just wondering if you ready for this shit, being married ain't as easy as we all make it look," D'Mari warned and his brother laughed cause he had to be joking. "I'm kidding nigga! You already know we go through our shit with them damn sisters. I just wanna make sure you ready for it."

D'Mani couldn't lie. His brothers weren't getting it easy messing with the Holiday sisters. But after all the time him and Stasia had been together and everything they'd been through, they may as well have been married because that's the life they were living and that's exactly what he told his brother.

"Shit we already living the married life, all we need is the paperwork."

"True, just know that the level of crazy goes up in that family once you say 'I do.' I think it's cause of Shirley's ass," he chuckled, but D'Mani knew he was only halfway kidding.

"Oh I done already seen it bro, trust me! The thing is though that I love her regardless and I love her son too. We're already like a big ass family, me, her, Kyler, and Imani. It's only right at this point for us to tie the knot," he shrugged, and D'Mari nodded his understanding. When they finally pulled up to speak to the pastor, the baby started fussing so D'Mari stayed behind to take care of her while D'Mani and Kyler went inside. They hadn't talked much about him marrying his mama, but he did know what his plans were. He must have been feeling a little nervous though because he felt like maybe he should say something else.

"So, you cool with me being yo step dad lil man?" Mani questioned Kyler, glancing down at him.

"I mean, ain't you already my step dad?" Kyler squinted up at him and shrugged.

"Already," D'Mani said, giving him a pound. It felt good knowing that he already considered him like *his dad*. Their relationship had come naturally and so had Imani and Stasia's.

Hours later as the sun began to set behind them, they all stood on the beach dressed in their all white, waiting for Stasia to come out. He was sure that at that point she knew what was happening. He nervously stood next to his brothers and Kyler with his hands clasped together in front of him.

"I wish she'd bring her ass on hell. It's too many kids over here to be watching!" Shirley snapped. She stood off to the side where the kids were inside of a small play yard.

"Aunty Shirley it's a whole pastor right here!" Alyssa sighed, covering her face with her hand.

"And? Wasn't y'all's daddy one too and we all know I ain't

care what came out my mouth with him around either and he was family! I don't even know this nigga!" she fussed, and everyone looked to the pastor who had shock written across his face. Thankfully, Drea cued the music right then as Anastasia came down onto the beach wearing a silk white dress that trailed behind her like she'd gotten it from a bridal shop.

She looked beautiful and D'Mani couldn't take his eyes off of her as she walked over the white rose petals that they laid out as an aisle. The smile on her face let him know that she was just as happy and excited as he was, even though she was only getting a small wedding. He planned on giving her something much bigger and better planned, but he was more than ready to make her his wife and he wasn't trying to wait. When it came time to recite vows, D'Mani just started talking since he hadn't had time to write any vows.

"Man we been through a lot ma, and it's crazy that we even made it here. You know that every day isn't going to be sunshine, but just know that I got'chu even when it's stormy outside. I can't imagine doing this shit with nobody but your crazy ass. Sorry Pastor. But you knew I wasn't letting no other nigga get at you. I'm so grateful for the love that you have shown Imani and for sticking it out with a nigga when things got complicated and chaotic. I love you and Kyler, and I know it's only right I spend the rest of my life showing you."

"D'Mani, I wasn't prepared for this, but I been ready to be your wife. You know that I can show my natural black ass... sorry Pastor... but I'm thankful that you can love me past my brand of crazy. I appreciate how hard you go for me and our family. I can't imagine life without you in it, so thanks being my husband, lover, rock, protector, counselor, voice of reason, and everything else for the good, bad, ugly, and petty times that will surely come. As long as I got you and our kids, I'm good and I know we will continue to rise above anything that comes our way. I love you so much and loving Imani came so natural to me because of that love. We're made for each other."

"Sholl in the hell is!" Shirley shouted from the side and Anastasia narrowed her eyes in her aunt's direction.

"Well in that case, I now pronounce you Mr. and Mrs. D'Mani Mitchell," the pastor announced, trying to hold back his laughter. "You may now kiss the bride."

D'Mani was more than ready to go on with their lives and he planned to live it to the fullest. He had a new wife and son he had to look after in addition to his daughter, and he planned on making them all happy no matter what. The rest of the vacation was spent honeymooning and enjoying family. Everyone enjoyed the shit because it would be time to get back to business soon and very soon.

✿ 36 ✿

SIX MONTHS LATER

"I'm getting so damn fat... UGH!"

J.R. glanced over at Lexi who pranced in the mirror, checking each angle in the full-length mirror.

He paused momentarily and admired his wife. Never in a million years did he expect to be married nor be a family man. Since making Lexi his wife and becoming a father, J.R.'s life had changed drastically; but minus the bullshit, life was great.

"Baby, you are the most beautiful woman in the world," he finally replied before walking over to her and wrapping his manly arms around her small frame.

"Nigga, I ain't say I was ugly... I said *fat*," she replied, smacking her lips.

"Well shit, I like my women BBW too," he joked before releasing his embrace.

Lexi spun around like a super hero and tried to hit him with a closed fit, but he was too quick for her.

"Look, I'm just playing but I need you to finish getting dressed... everyone is waiting on us."

After securing his black tie and the strap on her red

bottoms, the couple headed downstairs where everyone was waiting in the living room.

"Well ain't you fine Baby Holiday," Drea yelled from the bottom of the stairs as they made their way down.

"Shid, look who she get it from," Aunt Shirley bragged before placing Amir in his playpen.

"Thanks sister and you a fucking mess Auntie," Lexi chuckled.

"LEXI!" her mother yelled out before emerging from the kitchen.

"My bad ma, I ain't see you right there," Lexi smirked embarrassedly.

"Y'all ready to get this night started?" J.R. asked everyone as they headed towards the door.

Ms. Victoria and Yasmine were staying behind with the kids while the crew headed to an all-black-tie event. The gang tried their hardest to convince Shirley to stay but their words went in one ear and out the other, like always.

"I'm riding in the car with my Fav and J.R.," Shirley yelled as she struggled down Lexi's and J.R.'s driveway in her three-inch heels.

Once everyone was in their respective vehicles, J.R. pulled off right behind Corey and headed to the restaurant. The thirty-minute drive consisted of them smoking while Lexi and Shirley sang off key. J.R. handed his keys to valet before helping his wife and auntie out of the car. Once the gang was all together, they entered the restaurant together and was pleasantly surprised.

"Oh, Justin showed out!" Stasia said as she looked around the well-lit, beautifully decorated restaurant.

"Hell yeah, he shut shit down for family and friends. That's so dope," Lyssa added in as she too admired the settings.

J.R. couldn't front, the place did look nice. Justin rented

out a popular restaurant over in Duluth for his birthday dinner. He explained in detail on the invitation that it was an all-black-tie affair, which J.R. was excited about because he had never been to one.

"Looks like an open bar to me. I'll be back," Shirley said as she brushed past J.R in a hurry.

Already knowing how the night was going to end, J.R. grabbed Lexi's hand, pulling her to the center table. The table was decorated with black and gold fixtures from the plates to the seat cushions. Everyone took a seat where their name tag was placed and began to fraternize. J.R. checked his surroundings out of habit. Although their biggest problem had been eliminated, haters and jealous niggas still existed; therefore, he would never stop being cautious.

"Son."

J.R. felt a hand on his shoulder and a voice in his ear. Turning around, he was greeted by his father Justin.

"What up old man?" he said before standing to his feet and pulling Justin into a manly hug.

"Shit. Celebrating another year. How you been? I haven't seen you since you and Lexi picked Amir up from the house last week."

"Just getting back on track with this business shit. You good?" he twisted his head to the side and quizzed.

"I'm good son. I'm good." Justin smiled before grabbing the mic that was handed to him.

J.R. watched his Pops take a spot at the head of the table. He watched as he motioned with his head for the DJ to cut the music. When the crowded room finally simmered down, Justin cleared his throat before speaking.

"I wanna thank each and every one of you for being here with me today. I hold each and every person in this room close to my heart. As I celebrate a new year, I can't help but reflect on the past years, especially last year. Regardless of all the losses that I took..... and there was a lot.... the biggest *gain* was *my son*."

J.R. interest piqued at the mention of his name. Tuning in even more now, J.R. listened as Justin continued.

"I've been running a lucrative organization for over twenty-years and as you can see, I'm not getting any younger. So with that being said, I'm retiring and handing EVERY-THING over to my son, J.R."

The room erupted with congratulatory cheers and kind words. J.R. looked around at his immediate crew, each of them was just as shocked as him. When J.R. started selling weed as a kid just to cop the latest sneakers, he had no idea that he'll be in the position that he's in now. Since the beginning of the Rock Boyz, shit had been chaotic for him. So crazy that he considered giving up the game completely on several different occasions. He never wanted to put not only himself but the people he loved in danger again; but sitting there and staring at his father, it was in his blood. Although the Tessa's Cartel now belonged to him, J.R. knew none of that would be possible without his brothers.

"SPEECH.... SPEECCCCHHHHH.... SPPEECC-CCHHHHH!"

Everyone in the room chanted *"speech,"* forcing J.R. to stand up and take Justin's place on the microphone. Never being the one of many words, J.R. spoke from the heart.

"Gratitude Pops," He turned to Justin and said with a head nod before continuing.

"The NEW cartel has four leaders this time around. I couldn't do this shit without my brothers man. I love all y'all...."

"NIGGA, WHO GAY NOW?" D'Mani yelled from his seat, causing everyone to laugh, including J.R.

"Nah but on some real shit..... Let's get this mother-fucking money..... THE ROCK BOYZ FOR LIFE!"

THE END!!!

Made in the USA
Middletown, DE
08 September 2021